SWITCHBACK

A NICK TEMPLE FILE

JONATHAN DYER

CARTA

To the Men and Women of
Field Station Berlin
1983–1986

CHAPTER 1

SENDING A MESSAGE

For Steve Francis, the routine was simple: Kochstrasse, East Berlin, midnight. Dmitri gets the package and gives up an envelope. He'd done it half a dozen times in the year since Sputnik caused most of the West to lose its collective sanity. It's part of the game, and he'd been in the game since his days in the O.S.S. A freelancer. It's simpler that way. No official ties to the Company. It's also more lucrative, and he'd always had a nose for money. But it's also more dangerous. No back up. The Company isn't about to use assets to protect him, not as long as he insists on staying officially on the outside. Just the way he likes it. And then there's the routine. Another danger. He mentally resolves to bring up the need to shift the routine with Dmitri. But not tonight.

He leans against the building. The season's first snow can't be far off. He turns up his overcoat's collar against the night's chill, tugs his hat down low, pulls out his lighter, and lights a cigarette. Shit! Nasty German cigarettes. He left his ration card and his pack of Camels–solid American Camels–at the apartment before crossing over. He curses as he takes a drag. The smoke pinches his lungs, but he feels some satisfaction knowing that putting it out immediately is required. He'd have done it anyway. He keeps his face hidden, focused on the crushed cigarette.

The Soviet agent approaches as soon as the cigarette is out. Again routine, bordering on monotonous, bordering on foolish. Francis hears the footsteps, but keeps his head down until the footsteps stop. He peers from under the brim of his hat, and what he sees jars him.

"Where the hell is Dmitri?"

The Soviet closes in instantly. The click of a stiletto is all the time Francis has, and it isn't enough. Before he can turn or deflect the blow, the eight-inch, surgical steel blade punctures his heart.

"Never mind about Dmitri. No more questions for you." Francis groans weakly and slumps into the arms of the Soviet, who slowly, even gently, breaks his victim's fall to the ground. Steve Francis, anonymous Cold War hero, is dead within seconds.

The Soviet stands over the body as he meticulously wipes the blood from his stiletto with a bleached handkerchief that he lets fall on the dead man's face. He puts the stiletto into his overcoat pocket and steps silently away into the cold, anonymous night, never once looking back, certain of his success.

CHAPTER 2

MESSAGE RECEIVED

Agent Walker fights off the urge to sleep. He rubs his eyes and even slaps his face. Having a bacon cheeseburger and side of fries in the cafeteria at one in the morning seemed like a good idea at the time. Now he's paying for it. Five more hours until the day shift (known to his fellow shift workers as the day whores) takes over. He is sick of the graveyard, but he has to pay his dues. Once he gets four years in, once 1959 rolls around, he's in like Flynn. For now he just has to take it and not screw up. He rolls up the sleeves of his rumpled white shirt (how does it always look so bad just 3 hours into his shift?) and loosens his dark, thin necktie. Any movement, any effort, anything to stay awake.

He takes another sip from his coffee, rubs the sprouting stubble on his chin, and glances over at the row of five telex machines just beyond his desk. Traffic might start picking up any minute, now that the Commies are waking up. It is morning in Moscow, time for the routine intercepts. If he can manage to stay awake until the daily reports start coming in, he'll make it. Getting caught face down on his desk by some GS-13 is not considered to be a great career move. The wrench he feels in his stomach as the bitter black coffee hits the cheeseburger helps, but only for a minute. There's only so much the cuisine from the cafeteria can do for him. There's plenty it can do to him.

Walker can feel himself going under when one of the telex machines comes to life. Number 3–Berlin. Unusual, but not unheard of.

Walker takes another sip of his now lukewarm coffee, immediately regrets it, stands up, and walks over to the busily clacking telex, expecting nothing more than call sign changes and mid-range frequency targets.

He lifts the still-attached paper and reads as the telex rattles off encrypted source codes. Once the preliminaries are out, the message appears quickly. "Delta-27 sanctioned in Soviet sector, East Berlin, 0030 hours local, 31/10/58. No suspects. Body in custody of KRIPO. Advise."

Christ! Time to be alert. A dead agent. No, a murdered agent, and the body is already in the hands of the German police. Damn! Nothing routine about this shit.

Walker rips the message from the machine, reads it again to make sure the coffee, burger, fries, and late hour aren't all conspiring to make something out of nothing, and nearly runs out of the room in search of the night's duty officer for Soviet affairs.

CHAPTER 3

RINSE AND REPEAT

The narrow alley hosts a few cats looking for the nightly feast of slow, fatted, sewer rats. The cobblestone street, still slick from the recent rain, is deserted. Rene Bouldin, young, thin, and terrified, turns into the alley at a full sprint. The slap, splash, slap of his desperate stride sends cats and rats scrambling. He scans the dimly-lit alley for an open door as he runs. He looks desperately behind him expecting to be caught at any moment.

Seconds later his fears are realized as the high-pitched and strained whine of an engine revving high in low gear reverberates in the alley. Two assassins in a black, 1957 Fiat 1100 chase Bouldin. The sing-song cry of a police siren in the closing distance competes for sonic supremacy in the alley's sudden chaos.

A gunman leans out of the Fiat's passenger window. He ducks an overhang in the alley, straightens back up, and takes aim at the panicked Bouldin now less than 20 meters ahead. A flash explodes from the tip of his silencer, and a round slams into Bouldin's back sending him sprawling out of control face down onto the damp, filthy street.

The driver delivers the coup de grace by running over the nearly dead Bouldin, crushing his skull and any chance he had for survival. The Fiat speeds off, turning right onto the broad boulevard at the end of the alley, and disappearing into the labyrinth of Istanbul.

The police car, not more than five seconds behind, careens into the alley, siren still wailing. Its headlights catch the dead Bouldin just in time. The driver slams on the brakes, bringing the car to a wet, skidding stop inches from the maimed body. A member of Istanbul's finest jumps out and runs to the gory, lifeless figure. He stops and recoils when his eyes catch the damage done to Bouldin's former head. He throws his hat on the cobblestone pavement in disgust before starting the gruesome task of trying to identify the lump of former humanity, now nothing more than Cold War road kill, still warm and oozing, at his feet.

CHAPTER 4

TRICK OR TREAT

Cornell Bailey hasn't been home in more than 36 hours, yet his three-piece suit is meticulously neat. His appearance is a point of pride for him, and he holds in contempt those who let their, or the Company's, standards slip, even in the dead of night when no one else cares. His oak-paneled office has the prerequisite pictures of the President and Vice-President, an American flag in the corner, a large cherry wood credenza with assorted family portraits, and two stuffed leather chairs facing his desk. Other than the nod to his family, he hasn't made the office his own. The closet and personal bathroom speak to his position on the Company's food chain. He uses both to maintain a crisp appearance no matter the hour or the day, no matter how long it's been since he's been home.

He knows well that Special Assistants in most government offices come and go and there is no real point in getting comfortable. He worries that he has reached the peak of his career, a career still subject to the whim of a man who has been his senior for more years than he cares to admit, a man he does not particularly care for, a man whose existence is a growing source of bitterness for him. This peak is really not much more than an outcropping, half-way up the mountain, and he's stuck there.

He peers through his half-frames, studying the hastily constructed Berlin file with heightened attention. Time, date, names, location, weapon, all details that when properly understood might reveal more than the untrained eye can see.

The intercom on his desk buzzes and Bailey presses a flashing button.

"Yes?"

"Agent Walker has another telex, sir."

"Send him in."

He releases the button and goes back to reading the Berlin file. Walker, wide-eyed, rumpled, stubble on his chin, walks in. Bailey sets aside his disdain for the agent's appearance. More serious matters command his attention.

Walker hands Bailey a telex.

"Istanbul this time, sir. That's two in less than an hour."

"That'll be all, Walker."

Bailey enjoys being dismissive of underlings, although such a performance is often wasted when the only one present is the underling himself. Walker, hoping to chat it up a bit with one of the top men in the Agency, leaves disappointed.

Bailey reads the telex slowly, deliberately. He removes his half-frames and swivels in his leather chair to face the window above his credenza, to gaze into the darkness.

"Jesus. A helluva Halloween."

CHAPTER 5

THREE'S COMPANY

Herrengasse, Vienna, bustles with the weekday morning activity of those heading to work, and those whose job it is to see they get there on time, well-informed, and well-fed. Small, polite lines form in cafés, at newsstands, and at tram stops. The mild chill of late October holds out against the looming threat, the guarantee, of a deep, cold winter.

Roger Wooster–late 30s, British, and impeccably well-dressed–slides into the small café off the lobby of the Bristol Hotel. He has a woman on his arm. She is tall, thin, and likewise exquisitely dressed, even at this early hour. They both look more like part of Vienna's sophisticated opera aficionados than members of the daily workforce. Her Nordic beauty is unnoticed by the unflappable, hard-boiled commuter crowd, but it is appreciated by the café's staff. A glance followed by a nod from the headwaiter lets them know they are to seat themselves. They pick out a small, round, marble-topped table by the street window.

As Wooster sits, he motions to the waiter.

"Herr Ober."

A stout, middle-aged man with a pencil thin mustache, wearing a white shirt, a black bow tie, black pants, and a black apron, the recognizable garb of a Viennese café waiter, approaches.

"Speisekarte?" He offers Wooster and his companion a small breakfast menu, but Wooster waves the menus away.

"Zwei kaffe, bitte."

"Sofort."

The waiter nods and departs as Wooster unfolds his morning copy of *The International Herald Tribune*. His companion sets her purse on the table, glances around for the restroom, shifts once or twice in her seat and leans towards Wooster.

"Will you excuse me, darling? I need to powder my nose. Don't forget, two sugars."

"Of course," he replies without looking up from his paper.

"You're a dear," she purrs as she pats him on the knee.

She stands and casually walks away from the table as Wooster continues to read. She glances back to make sure his nose is still buried in his newspaper, and rather than turning right at the counter for the W.C., she turns left, leaving the café and heading briskly down the sidewalk towards the closest tram stop. She boards a waiting tram and in less than 30 seconds is lost in the crowded streetcar. The door closes and the streetcar pulls away into the busy morning traffic taking her safely out of range.

In the café, the waiter brings a small pitcher of coffee and two porcelain cups and saucers on a tray.

"Zucker oder sahne?"

Wooster closes his paper, looks at the tray and notices his companion's purse sitting on the table. A look of panic comes over his face. He springs from his seat, knocking over the waiter, just as a tremendous blast from the purse kills him and nearly everyone else in the café. The waiter, who was shielded from the blast by the shredded body of Roger Wooster, survives.

CHAPTER 6

SECOND CHANCES

Nick Temple–early 40s, short salt & pepper hair, a slight paunch–needs a shave. He got the call about four o'clock that morning, so no one other than Cornell Bailey would blame him for the stubble. He sits at his desk, his standard Company issue thin black tie already loosened, and the sleeves of his unstarched white shirt already rolled up. He reviews a folder, a TOP SECRET file, wondering why they called him.

His star had been descending for some time now, and what is sitting in front of him is as big as anything to come through the Soviet section for some time. Is this a setup? A test? A message that all is forgiven and he's back on the team? He ponders each of these questions, and a dozen others, as he studies the file. Berlin, Istanbul, Vienna. Berlin and Vienna are right up his alley. Istanbul's a bit out of his bailiwick, but if it's a Soviet job, then it could easily be related. His thoughts wander to Vanessa and the damage he did to himself in the Company, the general downgrading of assignments, the slow, but steady exodus of formerly close colleagues understandably distancing themselves from a tainted asset. He works to focus on the details of the file–Berlin, Istanbul, Vienna–but he is drawn back to his last night with her, after the Heraklion Gambit, and 24 hours after receiving an encrypted but direct edict from the Director to break off the relationship. They spent that last night yielding one last time to each other before walking away in the grey light of the Neapolitan dawn. A romp to remember, no doubt about it. And he paid for it, big time.

His desk phone rings; it rings a second time before penetrating his concentration. He picks up the receiver as he forces his mind to return to the potential catastrophe unfolding half way around the world.

"Temple, here. . . . I'm looking at the reports now. It's a fucking bloodbath over there. . . . No. . . . Johnson's got it too. . . . Yes, sir. Four p.m. in the briefing room. I'll be there."

Temple hangs up and continues to look through the file, shaking his head, wondering if the day will ever come when he can go 48 hours without gracing the wrong ear with the word "fuck."

CHAPTER 7

FOUR'S A CROWD

Niles Dubcek, 30-something, lean, and taut, even in his sleep, lies in a small bed in the middle of his sparsely furnished 4th floor studio apartment in Prague's historic center city. The city's first snow of the season falls gently outside his closed, floor to ceiling windows. The street is quiet, the small bit of human activity easily muffled by the accumulating snowfall. The poorly functioning radiator hisses slightly. A fully-loaded Walther PPK sits on a small nightstand next to Dubcek's bed, and next to it a travel alarm clock shows it's 2 a.m.

The door to the apartment, not more than 15 feet from the foot of Dubcek's bed, bursts open. Three intruders in black overcoats rush in. Dubcek is instantly awake and fully alert, his training and instincts his only hope for surviving the next 5 to 10 seconds. He reaches for the Walther PPK, rolls off the bed onto the floor and fires in the direction of the intruders, aiming center mass. One intruder is hit. He falls against the wall and slumps to the floor, alive, but groaning in agony from the hot, gushing hole in his intestine. The other two intruders pounce on Dubcek before he can get off another shot. Dubcek struggles fiercely, but the two men beat him senseless with their pistols and fists. Their orders are clear–terminate with extreme prejudice and without gunfire if at all possible, a sanction that sends a simple message of overwhelming brute force.

Once his assailants are certain Dubcek is unconscious, they drag him to the window and, without opening it, throw him through it onto the snow-covered sidewalk four stories below, the crash of the glass and the thud of Dubcek's body as it lands on the sidewalk destroying the snowy serenity of the street. There is no need for them to inspect their handiwork and they turn to leave.

One of the two intruders picks up Dubcek's pistol. He turns to his wounded comrade. With one hand, the dying man desperately clutches his midsection trying to keep his intestines from spilling into his lap, and with the other he begs for help. His plea is rejected without hesitation and he is executed by three quick shots to the head from the Walther PPK.

The executioner tosses the gun on the bed and the two survivors quietly leave the room less than a minute after entering.

CHAPTER 8

TEAM TEMPLE STARTS TO FORM

Bill Johnson, short, squat and muscular, still sporting the Marine crew cut from his days in the Korean War, carries a manila folder marked TOP SECRET, a mundane occurrence to be sure in these corridors. Over-classification is a running joke at the Agency and often the folders contain little more than sandwich and drink orders for another routine meeting. But this time the folder is far from routine and certainly no joke. Three highly-placed, valuable assets sanctioned in just about 24 hours. The body count itself is not remarkable, but the level of the assets and the chronological clustering both indicate the game is changing.

The whole Agency–an outfit that is supposed to be able to keep a secret–is buzzing about the unfolding disaster detailed in the file Agent Johnson carries to the Director's briefing room. Halfway there he stops at the office of Nick Temple.

Temple, who has managed a shave and a clean, pressed shirt for the meeting, opens the door before Johnson can knock, nods, and the two of them head off down the busy corridor.

"You clean up good."

"You know Bailey's not likely to listen to a thing I say. No need to antagonize him with a few whiskers and wrinkles."

"He'll listen. Delta wouldn't have sent it your way if they weren't interested in hearing what you have to say."

"You're probably right. Man, I've never seen anything like it,"

Nick offers.

"Three assets, all in the same day. Someone's sending us a message."

"Screw the message, someone's giving away the store." "No doubt about it," Johnson responds.

Having spent the last six hours going over the details of the files, the analyses, the clues, the remote and the likely possibilities, the wild guesses, and the concrete suppositions, they stand in agreement, an absolute necessity before briefing the Director and Special Assistant Bailey.

Nick knows this briefing could be his last if he screws it up. A nagging suspicion that he was chosen for this case for just that reason is hard to shake. He knows full well that the Company's political appointees aren't the only ones in the building constantly jockeying for position; that it's much easier to step over a body than go through one. He hopes Johnson is right, that he was assigned to the file because of his background, because of what he can bring to the table, and not out of some higher up's desire to see him make such a mess of things that he's finally put out to pasture. He regains his focus, telling himself there are only so many things within his control; the rest he'll leave to fate.

They stop at a set of wooden double doors with BRIEFING ROOM in plain block letters on them. A green light to the left of the doors indicates entry is permitted. They straighten their ties, pause and enter.

CHAPTER 9

READING TEA LEAVES

The briefing room is a small, carpeted amphitheater with seating for no more than 20 in three tiers. Seating for three, the Director, a stenographer, and the Special Assistant, is nearly always adequate. The Director prefers to keep the circle small. A lighted projection room sits in the back of the amphitheater, and a large screen covers the wall at the front.

The Director is already seated as Temple and Johnson enter. The Director is a well-groomed man in his late fifties; he looks like a bank executive at the pinnacle of his career in his three-piece, pin-striped suit. Normally unflappable, the knit of his brows betrays his deep concern as he reads a series of near-frantic cables from the Agency's European section chiefs.

Given his rural Midwestern origins, the Director surprised everyone when, as a young man, he parlayed an unusual academic flair for foreign languages into a full scholarship at Stanford University where he studied German and Russian. After graduation he secured a post in Charles Evans Hughes' State Department. He found diplomatic work tedious, but he used his time at Foggy Bottom to become an expert on the internal security apparatuses of Germany and the Soviet Union. When World War II broke out in Europe, he sought and received an appointment to the Army's Signals Intelligence Service, and he rushed to join the OSS when President Roosevelt brought it into existence in June of 1942. He spent much of the war in Istanbul, recruiting and training Austrian and German expats for missions deep inside Nazi Germany. He personally led his European protégés on half a dozen clandestine forays into Germany aimed at gathering vital intelligence for the State Department's post-war planning. When the Nazis got wind of his activities, they put a price on his head, a point of personal pride for him during the war and after. When the CIA was created in 1947, his appointment as Deputy Director of the Special Activities Division was roundly praised, as was his elevation to the post of D.C.I., Director of Central Intelligence, in 1954. By the time someone started killing American agents in Europe at an alarming rate, there was quite literally no man on the planet who had a clearer grasp of what was at stake than the Director.

A phone and an intercom speaker sit on a small table to the right of the Director. Special Assistant Cornell Bailey sits to the Director's left, and a young stenographer, in the tight skirt and equally tight blouse the Director prefers, sits in a chair just past the small table.

Johnson sits down in back on a simple folding chair outside the door to the projection room. Temple strides purposefully to a plain podium, with a microphone and small reading lamp attached, at the front-left of the amphitheater. He puts his folder on the podium and switches on the microphone and lamp.

The Director asserts his prerogative by speaking first.

"All right, Temple, I'll get right to it. What the hell is going on in Europe?"

Before Nick answers the Director of Central Intelligence, he seeks some clarification. He nods towards the stenographer.

"Someone want to tell me what's she doing here?"

The question is legitimate, but Nick instantly regrets having asked it. He might as well have asked, "Which one of you is covering his ass?"

Special Assistant Bailey puffs up, a favorite posture of his, to run interference. Years of playing the showy lap dog have made the roll almost instinctual. It's also his way of letting Nick know what he's up against.

"The President wants it all verbatim. He's not taking any chances. Any problem with that, Temple?"

His tone makes his disdain for Nick clear. He needn't have bothered, as no one in the room is under any illusions about Bailey's contempt for anyone whose personal life is a public, slow-motion train wreck. Like other hypocrites, Bailey considers a dalliance conducted without sufficient discretion to be evidence of a deep personality flaw.

"None at all. Just asking the question." Nick pauses, opens his file, and looks straight at the Director.

"We've been going over all the intel, sir. There's no question that someone is giving up our agents at a rate we've never before experienced. Okay, Walt, let's start," Nick says into the podium's microphone.

Walt, one of the Agency's many technicians whose job is to make the decision-makers' lives easier, nods from the projection room and flips a switch dimming the amphitheater lights. A grainy, black and white image appears on the room's screen. It's a photo of a middle-aged man, the one stabbed to death in Berlin, crossing a city street.

Nick glances at the file in front of him before starting. He's been over the facts so often in the last six hours that the file is almost superfluous. Still, he wants to get it right.

"Steve Francis. Murdered October 31st in Berlin. The first of three. Assailant unknown. He'd worked Berlin without incident since '45. A freelancer. Actually an accountant by trade. Had the nose of a bloodhound when it came to money. Gave us what we needed when Stalin died in '53 to stay in the game in Berlin."

The Director nods as he remembers '53.

"Any clues at all?"

"Not on the killer. He left behind a bloody handkerchief, but according to KRIPO, the blood all belonged to Francis. The m.o., stiletto to the heart, isn't one we've seen before in Berlin in this context. We're cross-checking it with other post-war sanctions in the East, but so far we haven't got a match. It may be a new player brought in from the Soyuz."

"Did you know him, Nick?

"Yes sir. I worked with him back in the OSS days. He always knew the risks, but it's tough to see it come to this. Next one, Walt."

The screen image changes to a black and white photograph of a young, thin man. He looks and is dressed like a beatnik, right down to the black turtleneck and black beret. He smokes a cigarette at a Parisian cafe. He is the man who was shot in the back before his head was flattened by the assassins' sedan in Istanbul.

"Number two. Rene Bouldin. Murdered October 31st in Istanbul. Again, assailant or assailants unknown. He came on board recently after being expelled from Algiers. He was keeping an eye on Soviet merchant marine activity in the Black Sea. Nothing too serious, but he was eager and thorough. His station chief notes he was being groomed for a move up. Remarkably bright, willing, and able. Tough shoes to fill."

The Director straightens up. "Why did you say assailants? More than one man in on it?"

"He was shot by someone in a car, most likely a driver and a shooter at a minimum. The round got him center mass, so it's unlikely it came from a driver. Istanbul police recovered a tag number and, later, the vehicle, but it's clean. This wasn't a jealous husband. These are highly compensated pros, who know what they're doing. Okay, Walt, next one."

The image changes to another black and white photograph– a head shot from a British passport–of a man in his late 30s, the man whose body was completely shredded in the bombing in Vienna.

"Number three. Roger Wooster. Murdered October 31st in Vienna. Wooster got rich working the lucrative Viennese black market after the war. He controlled some of the best counterespionage assets this side of the Iron Curtain. Honestly, with that much exposure, as long as he stayed in the game, it was only a matter of time. He knew it. He told me so over brandy and cigars in his club in New York six months ago. Admitted he liked the thrill of the chase, as he put it. Another nearly irreplaceable asset. His counterespionage contacts are likely to go to ground. We don't have a clear picture of the extent of his network, and likely never will. Next."

The image changes to a grainy photograph of a tall, thin, exquisitely-dressed woman walking down a Parisian sidewalk, and wearing a scarf and sunglasses. The scene is identifiable by the Art Nouveau entrance to the Parisian Metro.

"Wooster's killer is believed to have been this woman, Alexandra Simioneva, a KGB asset last seen in Vienna the day of Wooster's murder. She speaks fluent, unaccented French and English. How she got so close to Wooster is unclear. He may have been working to turn her and got careless. An eyewitness account from one of the few survivors of the blast at the café put her at Wooster's table moments before the explosion. She was not among the victims. There wasn't much left of Wooster, and no documents were recovered at the scene from what was left. Next."

A color photograph of the front of the former café shows the brutal effects of the blast.

"Someone survived that mess?" the Director asks incredulously.

"Wooster's waiter, it turns out, was among the few. A few pastry chefs in the back made it too. Wooster's body took the full brunt of the explosion, but also acted as a shield for the waiter. Last thing Wooster did for Queen and country. Damned lucky for us. The waiter lost some hearing for a while, and that's about it. He was able to give a statement at the scene. Really, quite incredible."

Bailey, who likes to interject himself in some way that shows his grasp of the big picture is superior to that of any agent, decides it's time to interject.

"Surely you have more than these fairly simplistic obituaries," he sniffs.

Temple gives Bailey a look of contempt, and is on the verge of letting him know what he thinks of Bailey's worth as a human. Johnson, who's seen that look before, jumps in to keep his friend from hanging himself.

"Ah, indeed we do, sir." As he talks, he takes a few steps down towards the stage to take their attention away from Nick.   "We've crosschecked the diplomatic traffic, our standard Stasi intercepts, and Soviet military SIGINT for the last three months. We found simultaneous references to a number of related Swiss financials, and we were able to pry some details out of the Swiss. They've been more helpful than usual. Seems they're pretty nervous about a full-scale blow up."

"What about an identity?"

The Director's well-known impatience is starting to show. Nick, who has calmed down, takes over.

"Negative, sir. We've got three account numbers that appear to be related, but we can't touch them. We can only trace major activity, and none of that is yielding a name."

The Director, who didn't rise to the level of the head of the most important intelligence agency in the world without having an almost unerring ability to read people, senses Temple is holding back.

"Quit being coy, Temple. Lay it out. What have you got?"

Nick hesitates. He knows this could be a make or break moment. The analysis is solid, he and Johnson have made certain of that, but it takes a field agent to see it, and both the Director and Bailey are many steps removed from the field. He has no choice. If he punts, they'll think he's gone soft.

"All right. Straight up. It's an American, sir. Likely someone at CIA or the Pentagon. State is out of the loop on enough of these assets that we can eliminate them."

The Director is staggered. A mole? On his watch? Knocking us out of a vital espionage theater? Heads have rolled for far less.

"Jesus! An American, Temple? Who would have the balls to play footsy with the Soviets in this day and age?"

Special Assistant Bailey feigns boredom to hide his shock at the news.

"Anything more specific you can give us gentlemen?"

Nick is nonplussed. He looks over at Bailey, pauses, and returns to address the Director before continuing.

"Walt."

A black and white image of a man stepping off an Aeroflot plane at Sheremetevo Airport in Moscow appears on the screen. The man is thin, tall, and angular. He wears a fedora and a dark, high quality, three-piece suit. He looks like a westerner conspicuously out of place in Moscow's busiest airport. After a few seconds, Walt switches the slide to a close up of the same shot. Nick lets the image soak in for a moment before he once again addresses the small group.

"It appears that the operation is being run out of KGB in East Berlin. Our analysis leads us to conclude that this man, their operational chief, Vasily Ivanovitch Malenkov, has day-to-day responsibility, but we doubt it was his idea."

The Director interrupts. "Why is that?"

Johnson, seeing his chance to bolster the hypothesis' bona fides, to show the team is behind this analytic leap, joins in.

"It's not his usual style. He likes to think that he views the world through the prism of a gentleman. Espionage is an elaborate ballet to him, and, like classical ballet, he sticks to clearly defined forms and plot lines. This series of events is too far outside of those lines for him."

The sophistication of Johnson's analyses is legendary at the Company, primarily because they rarely square with his ex-Marine image, an apparent contradiction Johnson consciously cultivates. Nick plays tag team as Johnson pauses.

"Besides that, he's not high enough up to have put this together on his own. The orders have to be coming from Moscow, but we're fairly confident East Berlin is ground zero for the operational effort. In spite of Malenkov's gentlemanly demeanor, he's a true believer, and would strangle his mother if ordered to by Moscow. Walt."

A color image of the Soviet Trade Mission Building in East Berlin appears on the screen as Nick continues.

"Malenkov runs a satellite operation out of this building at 77 Albrechtstrasse in East Berlin. It's thinly staffed. We've had a double agent in that building before, and our best intel indicates that, in addition to being a sort of private office for Malenkov, it is used from time to time both as a safe house for KGB assets and as an interrogation center. There may be some military assets, perhaps a dozen soldiers, stationed there as well, but even that presence is surprisingly low key. Malenkov is likely running the operation from this building. If Moscow has delegated operation control, he's the only one outside of Moscow with the pull and the scope of contacts who can make it happen."

"What about the building? Any schematics on the interior?"

Temple is prepared for the Director's question. Another agent might have skipped the detail. But Nick, a veteran of these briefings, has it covered. He knows that even the appearance of being unprepared can kill a career. With his own career on life support, he has to be better than the rest.

"No, sir. Walt?"

An incomplete overhead drawing of the Trade Mission Building's ground floor appears on the screen.

"The Soviets have never made a habit of getting building permits from their East German hosts. As you can see from the slide, we know very little about how the interior is configured. What we do know is that immediately inside the front door there is a reception area that also houses monitors for a closed-circuit security system. Beyond the reception desk is a stairwell and, on the same floor, a secured door. As you face the reception area to your left is a hallway about 30 feet in length. There are adjacent restrooms for men and women shortly before another security door at the end of the hallway. We believe Malenkov's office is beyond this second security door, and that there are billets, a cafeteria, and perhaps analysis shops on the three floors of the building. If there are underground floors housing anything besides the normal physical plant to support a building of this size we are unaware of their existence."

Special Assistant Bailey thinks Temple and Johnson have gone too far, that their jump to Malenkov is unsupported. He interrupts.

"This is all speculation."

"We prefer to call it analysis." Nick's sarcasm is just shy of insubordinate.

The Director steps in to separate the two. "All right, all right. Anything else, gentlemen?"

"I'm afraid not. We've got some more digging to do, but the trail goes cold when we get back to the U.S."

Johnson's frank admission is his way of taking one for the team. If the analysis is thin, the Director will remember that it was Johnson who had the last word.

The Director switches into "get it done" mode.

"Look, if we don't get a line on who this is, and do it in a goddam hurry, we're going to have to do a massive reallocation of assets that will disrupt collection for at least a year."

Nick, anxious to cure any lingering effects of his sarcasm, weighs in.

"Clearly that's what the Soviets envision at a minimum, sir."

The Director ponders Nick's last statement. The room is silent as they all wait for some direction. Suddenly, the intercom speaker next to the Director's seat buzzes startling them all. The Director flips a switch on the speaker.

"Cheryl, this had better be good."

The voice of the Director's personal assistant announces ominously, "I've got the Prague station chief on the encrypted line, sir. He says it's urgent."

The Director looks around, a look that says, "We all know what's coming."

"Put him through."

The Director flips the speaker switch back to the off position, picks up the receiver to the phone next to him, and pushes a flashing button on the phone.

"Harry? What is it?"

The Director's face darkens as he listens.

"Thanks, Harry. We're working the problem. Put your report in the pouch. Stay off the telex for now."

The Director hangs up and exhales deeply.

"That was Taft, our man in Prague. They lost their top man last night. Thrown to his death from his fourth story apartment."

The room is silent as each man in the room considers the impact, on the nation's security and on their own careers, of the latest casualty.

"Gentlemen, the President has given this top priority. I want some answers, and I want them yesterday, understood? Cornell will see to it that you get whatever you need. By God, we've got to stop this or we're not going to have any assets left to reallocate."

Johnson and Temple nod. They know the Director has nowhere else to go with this at the moment so he's going to stick with them. The briefing's a tactical success, but now they're on the line. If they're wrong about Malenkov, they'll both be reading translated documents from the Chinese Communist revolution until they retire.

"That's all, gentlemen."

Johnson and Temple leave. Bailey motions for the stenographer to leave as well. Bailey and the Director watch silently, appreciatively, as she packs her equipment and walks out. Walt turns the light out in the projection room leaving the Director and his Special Assistant alone to ponder the fate of America's Eastern European intelligence network.

"You think they're up to it, sir?"

"I worked with both of them right after Korea. Absolutely."

"Frankly, sir, you know as well as I do that Temple's slipping. His divorce was ugly and expensive. I'm not sure he's recovered."

"We're not asking him to do any field work. He knows the drill on the analysis. He'll be fine. Besides, divorce is a fact of life. Why should Temple's be different?"

"Bills. More than usual. Kids in college. A wife that lives high on the hog on the west coast. He got taken to the cleaners. The cost of infidelity, I suppose. The judge really shoved it to him. I wonder what he'd have done to him if he'd known the indiscretion was with a double agent. Sloppy."

"That was best handled internally."

"But the bills, sir. It makes him a perfect counterespionage target."

"Bills are one thing. They didn't start piling up until the affair was over. There's no question he's a Company man."

"Certainly not until that business about his brother's death. The talk around the water cooler is he blames the Army."

"I'm not buying it, Cornell. A man that's served his country as long as Temple has doesn't go south just like that. He's as by the book as anyone in this building. My only concern is his age. Does he still have what it takes?"

"I just thought we should have the conversation, sir."

"Of course. That's fine. Kyle Richardson's part of his team, right?"

"Correct."

"That should help. He was a recon Marine in Korea and is still tough as nails. Look, keep a discreet eye on Temple just the same. Nothing too heavy, he'd likely pick it up anyway. Just keep your ear to the ground."

The two men, without another word, leave the room, each burdened by the uncertainty of the next 24 hours.

CHAPTER 10

IF THE SHOE FITS

Kyle Richardson never really left the Marine Corps. His haircut and physique outwardly betray a quiet and determined sense of duty and loyalty so often characteristic of men who have served under fire. As Nick Temple and Bill Johnson pore over boxes of documents late into the night with their ties loose and their sleeves rolled up, Kyle Richardson works alongside them, tie up, sleeves down and buttoned, looking as if he expects an inspection, one he would pass with flying colors, at any minute. Unlike so many who are driven by an intense personal discipline, Richardson never lets it color his view of others. The standards he internalized in the Corps are now his own as if he had been born with them. If others live by a different standard, it is not for him to say they live in error.

Bill Johnson needs a break. He gets up and stretches his muscular frame. He lets the others know what he has been thinking to himself for the last six hours of this drudgery.

"There's only so far this paper is going to take us. We need to get on the ground, work it from the inside. Our rat is a smart rat. Every trail is a dead end, and I don't see it getting any better."

Richardson, ever mindful of the task at hand, responds.

"I'll finish these reports. We've got to at least tie up what we have."

Nick, whose mind has wandered for an hour or so, decides to

drop his bombshell.

"I'm going to bring Vanessa in. She has banking contacts that might unlock these accounts."

He waits for the others' reaction. Johnson is first to speak up.

"Not a great idea, Nick," he says simply.

"I'm ready to listen to better ideas."

"I don't trust her."

"No one does, but she's the only asset I can think of that we can pull off the street without causing a stir. Besides, I'm already divorced, so where's the harm?"

"Harm's already done," Johnson, who is not ready to let go, reminds Temple.

"Fuck you."

"I'm just saying, Nick."

"Well don't say. Forget it. Let's get back to work."

Johnson shrugs, sits back down, pulls a file from one of the boxes, opens it and starts reading. Nick, as the team's leader, knows he needs to smooth over the minor spat.

"Besides, what would I want with a woman like that when I can spend all the quality time I want with you assholes?"

They all laugh lightly before digging back into the documents.

Richardson, loyal as always, comes to the aid of the team's unofficial leader.

"Vanessa might not be a bad idea, but we should clear it with the Director first. SOP, right?"

"The kid's right, Nick."

"I doubt he'll go for it. She's company poison since they found out about her affair with Malenkov."

Johnson and Richardson look at each other. Richardson shrugs.

"Don't kid yourself, Nick. That's not what put her on the radar screen around here," Johnson counters.

"I didn't think you'd fall for that."

"I'll be honest with you, Nick. I don't like going behind the Director's back. If you're going to contact her, it's gotta be through channels. That's all I'm saying." Richardson's loyalty often expresses itself in ways that keeps his friends out of trouble, a core belief of his.

"All right. I get the message. I'll pitch it tomorrow. All he can say is no and then we're no worse off than we are now."

They all nod in agreement before they dig back into the documents, collectively thinking that the life of a CIA agent isn't always as exciting as those outside of the Company are led to believe.

CHAPTER 11

FOOL ME TWICE

The Director is not pleased. Bailey warned him that Temple might not be all there anymore, and this jarring request seems to confirm that. But he's stuck. He has to act quickly, he has to be seen as nimble, able to respond to a crisis, or the President might start looking around for a new D.C.I. Even a day's delay would cause eyebrows to be raised in offices where a raised eyebrow can have serious consequences. He started down this road and now he's stuck.

Nick knows the Director's boxed in, but that's not why he makes this request. He, too, is out of options, and can ill afford to be seen throwing up his hands. He was brought in right from the get go on this one, a final chance to prove he shouldn't be put out to pasture. He has to make this work.

"She's got some contacts we can't touch without her," Nick says into the speaker phone on his desk as Richardson and Johnson take in the conversation. There's a pause before the Director responds, before he raises the red flags. Nick would have preferred a face to face meeting to get a read on the Director as the conversation unfolded, but a conference call was all his boss's schedule would allow.

"What about Malenkov?'

"It's over for them. We have no charted activity between them for more than two years. Besides, if we're right, Malenkov's the key to this. It might not hurt if he thinks we're closing in. A little pressure can pay big dividends."

"All right. Put her to work, but keep a tight leash on her. Keep her on a need to know basis, and for Christ's sakes, keep it in your pants this time."

A dial tone replaces the Director's annoyance. Nick calmly pushes a button on the phone killing the dial tone. He shakes his head and says, to no one in particular, "Jesus. One mistake in almost 20 years."

"Not a small mistake," Johnson reminds him.

"That's what the judge said."

Nick and Bill stare at each other tensely for a moment. Bill never tires of acting as Nick's conscience, of saying the things that need to be said to keep his friend in line. Nick's trouble usually starts when his good friend is not around, when his instant and biting counsel is not a part of the daily routine.

Nick chuckles.

"I promise I'll keep all my clothes on this time. Scout's honor."

"Meet her outside. Less chance of anything happening that way," Richardson chimes in.

"Right you are. All right, let's get to work. When we find her, and there's no guarantee we will, what do we want from her, how do we want it from her, and what are we willing to pay? We need a plan, boys. Meet me back here right after lunch."

The two get up to leave, but Johnson stops.

"Nick, sorry about the comment. I'm just trying to look out for you, buddy."

Nick, as always, is touched by his friend's loyalty, the sort of loyalty that means he'll always tell him exactly what's on his mind, even if Nick doesn't want to hear it.

"Forget it. You're right, but it's over, and I can handle it. Like I said, scout's honor."

Johnson and Richardson nod and leave, both of them unconvinced, but willing to give their friend and colleague, a man who has devoted his life to his country and who has asked for little in return, the benefit of the doubt.

CHAPTER 12

SQUARING AN ACCOUNT

An aging Short Solent four-engine seaplane lands on the crystal blue water of a secluded harbor in the Cayman Islands. Its engines strain, accelerating at first, and then dropping to an idle, as it taxis up to a small finger pier running out from the land. A convertible Mercedes-Benz 300SL roadster, its top down, is parked near the land end of the dock. Its owner, a short, fat man in a tight-fitting, tropical-white, three-piece suit, stands out on the pier. The midday sun's effects can be seen in the ring of sweat at the top of his tight collar. He braces himself against the blast from the props as the pilot expertly guides the Solent to the end of the pier.

The door of the seaplane opens and out steps Vanessa Porter–middle-aged, leggy, and beautiful, looking as if she is about to go on a high fashion shopping spree at the House of Chanel. The fat man wipes his brow, stuffs his handkerchief in his back pocket, and scrambles to meet her. He takes her hand as she steps onto the pier.

"Why do you ask so much of me, Vanessa?" he shouts over the roar of the twin engines.

Vanessa caresses his fat cheek to reassure him. He shifts his feet nervously, worried about his skin, but unwilling to appear as a complete coward in front of this beautiful woman.

"What did you find?"

"It's not good. I don't know what it means, but I'm sure it's not good."

"You needn't worry. There's no way to trace it to you."

"You're either mad or a liar. Of course it can be traced to me. This cancels my debt, Vanessa. No more. My heart can't take it."

"You're a dear. All right, we're even then if what you have can help me." Vanessa is not ready to surrender his obligation to her entirely.

"I can give you a name."

"I need paper. I have my own credibility problems. I know you, Heinrich. Whatever you have is on paper, so you might as well give it to me."

Heinrich gets his handkerchief back out to wipe the profuse perspiration from his brow. Once his brow is temporarily dry, he touches it lightly with his other hand to see if his pale, banker's skin is getting burned. He stares at Vanessa for a moment. He knows if it hadn't been for her the home office in Zurich would have sacked him after the mess in Algiers, but he wants no more of her and her intrigue. He relents, pulls a business envelope from his suit jacket breast pocket, and hands it to her.

"He'd like to talk to you personally. You know how these men are, convinced of their powers of observation. Why don't you come with me? I can have you home before you're missed. You really shouldn't go back to work today. You're much too agitated to be any good to anyone."

"You're mad. I'm already missed, and I've risked more than I should by coming here at all. No, Vanessa. This is it. My account is clear. You should forget my name. I will treat yours as if it is the name of a dead woman."

"Such drama, Heinrich. You really need to learn to relax."

She kisses him on both flabby cheeks, turns, and gets back on board the seaplane with the envelope in her hand. The plane's engines accelerate and it immediately departs from the dock.

Fat Heinrich scurries back to the convertible. He fumbles with the door, his agitation making the simplest tasks near impossible. He finally manages to get behind the wheel, wipe his soaked brow once more, start the engine, and drive away, tires skidding furiously in the crushed shells and sand as he floors the accelerator. Overhead he sees the seaplane lift off and climb to the north and west. It's the last thing he sees before the searing white flash produced by the detonation of the bomb under his seat obliterates him and his car on the sandy, remote road.

As the seaplane continues to bank, Vanessa watches Heinrich's car explode into a deadly ball of flame.

"Now, Heinrich. Now your debt is repaid, you pig." She vaguely, even fatally, wonders if the seaplane is next.

CHAPTER 13

THE MAN BEHIND THE CURTAIN

Colonel Yevgeny Roznecheko–the stout, some would say plump, uniformed KGB chief political officer for its Western Section–sits at his desk barely reading a file. He is in his late 50s, and he's a survivor of revolution, civil war, famine, world wars, and countless purges. Indeed, more than merely surviving, as millions of Russians could have claimed, Roznechenko managed to turn each cataclysmic world event to his personal advantage. And now, as he daydreams about retirement, as his thoughts turn freely to his wife's eventual arrest, exile, and execution, as he conjures images of his golden years on the warm beaches of the Crimean in a Communist Party villa he and his mistress have already selected, he is certain of one thing: his future in the byzantine world of the Soviet Union's Communist Party is as secure as it can be. He has spent most of the last 40 years, when others were attending to petty matters such as the Ukrainian famine or the German invasion, securing his present and future through a vast web of connections, bribes, dossiers, and fawning underlings. He feels destined to die peacefully, a boast not many around him can claim with any certainty.

His daydreaming is interrupted by the entrance of Vasily Malenkov. Malenkov is smoking. He wears a dark two-piece suit with a white handkerchief in his breast pocket. He is immaculately groomed, and, to Roznechenko's disgust, his manners are impeccable. As such, it is his duty to speak first.

"Good morning, Comrade Colonel."

"Good morning, Vasily Ivanovitch. Please sit down."

Malenkov sits in one of the two chairs in front of the Colonel's desk. Both chairs are upholstered in fine Italian leather, a detail sharply familiar to the urbane Malenkov. He takes another drag on the cigarette letting the smoke escape from his mouth before pulling it in through his nostrils.

"Our American friend gave us another name. This one in Copenhagen." Roznechenko is alert to any reaction from Malenkov to the news of imminent bloodshed. He knows that murder is part of his colleague's résumé, and that Malenkov's gentlemanly demeanor is a thin veneer for a cold-blooded killer. In spite of that, Roznechenko is still on the lookout for a weakness that might be of use to him someday.

Malenkov knows to remain nonplussed and direct. He gestures towards the ashtray on Roznechenko's desk.

"May I?"

"Of course."

Malenkov extinguishes the cigarette. As he does, he asks, "And?"

"Of course, we will act on it, like the others."

Malenkov decides to risk an observation.

"That's five in as many days. How long do you think the Americans will stand for this?" The decision is an uncharacteristically poor one.

"The Americans are cowards!" Roznechenko thunders. "They have no stomach for this! We must build on our successes. We crushed the Hungarians, the Americans showed their cowardice in the Suez, Sputnik circles the globe! The Soviet Union is marching forward, planting the banner of socialism in frontiers never before imagined, yet you worry about the spineless Americans! Sometimes all you have to do is break wind and the Americans move an entire fleet. And then what? Nothing! They do nothing!" Roznechenko pounds his hands on his desk as he rises from his chair during his well-rehearsed tirade.

Malenkov, who remains calm throughout the explosion that has likely been repeated at any number of meetings, recovers from his ill-considered observation.

"Of course, Comrade Colonel. I simply wonder when they will begin to strike back and who the targets will be. Tit for tat, as it has always been. You'll agree, of course, we have assets to protect that are useful for, shall we say, our larger aims."

"The old rules are gone. It is a new era. The Americans are in no mood for World War III, and that is what they will risk if they retaliate."

Roznechenko returns to his seat, whatever effect his having risen and lectured Malenkov having subsided.

Malenkov knows that if there are "new rules" then Roznechencko most likely has a keen understanding of them. The Colonel's survival and uninterrupted ascendance are legendary in KGB and Communist Party circles.

Malenkov decides he must save some face.

"But it is the same game."

Roznechenko once again rises from his chair, slowly this time partly out of deference to his portly condition, and partly for effect, to indicate that he, Comrade Colonel Yevgeny Roznecheko, an official hero of the Soviet Union, a decorated veteran of the Great War for the Fatherland, decides when meetings are over.

"I only told you of this as a courtesy. You will need to take whatever precautions you deem necessary. Belyofsky has the information as well and has been ordered to see that the sanction is carried out."

Malenkov stands up and, with an overly polite gesture, almost a bow, that he knows will irritate Roznechenko, he defers.

"Of course, Comrade Colonel. And I am most grateful for the courtesy of this meeting. I bid you good day."

"Remember, Vasily Ivanovitch, you are to take those actions you think prudent in light of this development."

Covering his ass, as always. Maybe I can make him squirm, Malenkov thinks to himself.

"What would you have me do, Comrade Colonel?"

"Why are you asking me how to do your job? Enough!"

Malenkov, certain that Roznechenko will provide nothing concrete so that in the event the operation goes south he can claim he ceded authority and was all along unaware of operation's clumsy particulars, sees no point in persisting. He clicks his heels, nods slightly, turns, and exits.

Roznechenko sits again and, with little else to do that day, returns to dreaming of the languid nights on the Black Sea waiting for him at the end of his long, dark career.

CHAPTER 14

THE FIFTH JACK

The November Danish night is predictably frigid. A brisk wind off The Sound drops the temperature well below freezing. In spite of the weather, Copenhagen's popular Tivoli Gardens are crowded and noisy. A man leans on one of the massive supports of the Gardens' famous wooden roller coaster. His brimmed hat is pulled down low over his eyes and he wears a heavy wool overcoat. He pulls a pack of cigarettes out of his breast pocket, and taps it twice to extract a cigarette. He puts the unfiltered cigarette in his mouth, replaces the pack, gets a lighter out of his pants pocket, lights the cigarette, and takes a drag. He examines the smoldering cigarette briefly before dropping it to the pavement and crushing it with his shoe. He puts his hands in jacket pockets to keep them warm, the small Beretta in his right pocket a recent addition.

To his right, six skinny young Danes huddle together against the cold. They affect the look of American beatniks: tight black clothes, scraggly beards for the men, more black clothes and long, straight hair for the women, a beret or two, and cigarettes all around. Cool and contemptuous, and all of them blonde. It is hard to tell one from the other. They smoke and chatter casually, aimlessly, seemingly oblivious to anything outside of their small circle. They laugh in unison at the nonsense of their inside jokes. The tallest male puts his cigarette out and fidgets, looking around over the top of his companions.

A train of cars from the roller coaster approaches. The noise quickly becomes overwhelming. The tallest Dane looks away from the group and over his shoulder. He reaches under his overcoat. As the cars are directly overhead, as the noise is at its peak, a muzzle flash appears from the group to the smoking man's right. A round slams into the smoking man's skull just behind his right eye, ripping through his frontal lobe and taking brain, hair, skin, and skull with it as it exits above his left ear. His death is instantaneous; his body collapses and falls to the ground in the shadow of the support. The young Danes put out their cigarettes and disperse as the noise from the roller coaster cars fades and the dead man's blood pools on the frozen ground.

CHAPTER 15

DEAD END

Time to check on Nick. Johnson rings the doorbell again and looks at Richardson.

"Bailey said he was in, right?"

"Right. Try again."

Johnson is about to ring the buzzer a third time when he hears Nick from inside.

"It's open."

Richardson and Johnson walk in wearing overcoats wet from the rain, brush the rain off their hats, and hang their hats and coats on a bamboo coat rack in the corner next to the front door. Temple sits on his couch, his feet on the cheaply furnished apartment's coffee table, a highball in his hand, watching a small black and white TV. The TV's sound is turned all the way down. The living area of his small, cluttered apartment consists of a kitchen set off from the living/dining room by a counter that doubles as a bar. Private schools and alimony leave little for housing expenses. It's more than enough for a man whose tastes are, as his ex-wife once said at a mind-numbing, Washington, D.C., party, "bleakly utilitarian."

Johnson eyes the highball. "You got another one of those?"

"In the kitchen. Help yourself. You know the drill."

Johnson walks into the kitchen and grabs a glass. He throws a couple of ice cubes from a plastic bucket on the worn linoleum counter into the glass, picks up an already open bottle, and pours himself a bourbon on the rocks. Richardson sits down in an easy chair to Nick's left.

"How 'bout you, Kyle?"

"No thanks, Nick. Someone's gotta mind the store."

"Suit yourself."

Johnson comes in to the living area with his drink and sits next to Nick on the worn out sofa.

Nick feels a surge of sarcasm. "All right, I'll bite. What's the good news?"

"There isn't any. Bailey told us you got a call about Copenhagen."

"Yep. That's five in a week. Christ."

Johnson takes a swig of cheap bourbon, winces, and wipes his mouth with the back of his hand.

"You see the dispatches?"

"A courier brought them over an hour ago. Nothing."

"Someone's laughing at us," Richardson interjects.

"And killing our friends, let's not forget."

Temple takes a long drink. Richardson watches the silent TV. Johnson decides to get down to business.

"We have to see the Director again tomorrow afternoon."

"You go. I have a date."

Johnson nearly drains his drink.

"Suit yourself. It's your funeral."

"Not to worry. It's all approved and strictly platonic. Anything new from that last batch of financials?"

Johnson shakes his head. "Just clutter. Man, I can hardly see straight from all that reading."

"Good time to get behind the wheel."

Johnson gulps down the rest of his drink and gets up.

"No. Now it's a good time to get behind the wheel. I've got to take off. I haven't seen Peggy and the kids in three days. Kyle?"

"I'm gonna stick around and watch TV with Nick here. I'll see you tomorrow, bright and early."

"You two behave yourselves."

Johnson turns to leave.

"What the hell kind of trouble can I get into with a boy scout?"

Richardson moves over to the couch, picks up a newspaper off the coffee table and opens it. As he pretends to peruse a couple of columns of print, he says, "That's the point, Nick. That's exactly the point."

CHAPTER 16

NICK ON A DATE

The cold, grey, late afternoon sky makes the nation's capital look as if winter has arrived early. For a southern city, D.C. has more than its share of bitter November days. This is one of them. The trees have lost their leaves; the wind kicks debris about; people walk briskly to cars, to doors, to anything out of the cold. Nick Temple, sporting a day's beard and superfluous sunglasses, sits by himself on one end of a park bench near the Capitol building. Vanessa Porter, carrying a folded newspaper under her arm, approaches and sits down at the other end of the bench. She is bundled up against the cold and also wears sunglasses. Nick knows he's being tailed. There's no need for disguise, but old habits are hard to kill.

They both look straight ahead.

"When did you get in?"

"About an hour ago. I'm surprised you have to ask. Don't you have someone watching me anymore, Nicky?"

"Not for some time now."

"If you're telling the truth then I'm disappointed. I thought I was more important to you than that."

"Believe it or not, we trust you."

Vanessa laughs. "I don't believe you. You don't even trust yourself, Nick."

"All right, I'm a liar. No one trusts you. Let's cut the bullshit.

What have you got?"

"Not much. I'm afraid you might be wasting your time. You already suspected it is an American. Much more than that, I can't tell you."

Nick looks at her. As beautiful as ever.

"What happened to your trust? These are my friends too, Nick."

Nick looks away; he has to.

"You have too many friends."

"Impossible."

"Tell me I didn't fly you in so you could tell me what I already know. You said you have more."

"I do, but I like to make you squirm."

"Let the record reflect that I'm squirming." More than she would ever know.

Vanessa puts the newspaper on the bench between them. Nick, after a pause, picks up the newspaper and opens it. He unfolds, and reads a small piece of paper that was tucked inside.

"Damn."

"He recently opened an account in the Caymans."

"What?"

"It's supposed to be for his mistress, but there's too much money in it for that cheap whore."

'How much?"

"One point five million."

"You have proof?"

"On paper? No. The account can't be traced, but I know the

bank's director."

"I want to talk to him."

"That won't happen, Nicky. I already asked him. I can't say that I blame him. Anyone finds out he's talking to you and he and his bank are ruined. When I asked him he ran like a scared fat little boy. What are going to do about your traitor?"

"No one else is talking either. The killings are having an effect. No one feels safe."

"Well, now you can put an end to it."

"It's too thin. I don't mean to sound unappreciative, but there's not much I can do with it. He's too shrewd and too well-connected. He'd wriggle out of it in a New York minute, and that'd be it for me. Strike two. This ain't baseball. Two's all you get."

"Why be subtle?"

"Murder?"

"Such a harsh word. Don't you prefer sanction, or at least termination?"

"Impossible. He's too high up. The whole thing would go public, and if they start looking for a sacrificial lamb, like I said, that'd be it for me. You sure I can't talk to your banker?"

"I'm afraid you'd find the conversation a trifle one-sided."

"I saw that in the chatter. That was your guy?"

"No one will miss him."

"Who ordered it?"

"I have no idea. Why do you think I know so much more than your entire government?"

"Just asking the questions. Comes with the territory."

Vanessa stands up. "It's your puzzle, Nicky. I can't give you all the pieces. Maybe you'll have to shake it out of the Russians yourself."

"You know more, don't you?"

Vanessa steps in front of him and puts her hand on his cheek. "You used to shave for our dates."

Nick affects a lack of interest. He promised the fellas, and he is trying hard to keep the promise.

"Get back to Berlin. I may need you."

She removes her hand from his cheek and looks away.

"There was a time when hearing that would have given me a thrill."

They stare at each other for a moment.

"When's your flight?"

"It's the red eye to London."

Temple gets out a pen and writes on the back of the piece of paper Vanessa gave him. He hands her the slip of paper.

"My place is a mess. It's impossible to get good help these days."

Vanessa reads the piece of paper, folds it, and puts it in her coat pocket. She walks away leaving Temple sitting on the park bench. He picks up the newspaper, gets up, walks a few steps to a garbage can, tosses the newspaper in and keeps walking. He thinks about having a couple of pops at the Green Lantern, a dive less than half a block from his apartment. But he has to be honest with himself: there isn't enough bourbon in the entire state of Kentucky to wash away what he's feeling right now.

CHAPTER 17

I'M WATCHING

Cornell Bailey sits at his desk and looks through a folder containing an array of black and white pictures of the meeting between Nick Temple and Vanessa Porter. Each 8 x 10 has a time and date hack in the lower left corner. Viewed in sequence they provide a moment by moment pictorial recreation of the approved meeting. Two agents, neither a particular Nick Temple fan, and both aware of the Special Assistant's clout, sit in the chairs in front of Bailey's desk. Bailey has seen enough and closes the folder.

The pictures tell less than they might. Without audio it's impossible for anyone to know precisely what transpired between Nick and Vanessa. Audio equipment on short notice would have given their presence away. Nick still has a few friends left tucked away in the Agency's corners. Besides, it's likely Temple knew he was being watched, so it's just as likely that audio would not have revealed anything. A careful, seasoned field agent can pass the most complicated of information with the simplest of conversations, something that looks like nothing more than a chat about breakfast, or the weather, or how the Washington Redskins are doing this year. But Temple had screwed up before. Maybe he's lost his edge. Audio would have provided some clue.

Bailey feels his frustration mounting as he contemplates the incomplete report, but he is careful to keep his uneasiness internal. Spooks are trained to detect mood changes and these two generic agents in front of him are certainly no exception. Bailey has to be cautious; any shift, any slip will be the object of water cooler speculation as surely as if it were part of the morning briefing. Or worse, an ambitious agent could take his thoughts higher up, to a bureaucratic rival, producing a red flag that could ruin a career. Bailey has played that game himself and he is well aware of the deadly consequences.

"Okay. Keep on him. I want a new report on my desk each morning. That'll be all, gentlemen."

The agents, without further comment, stand up simultaneously and leave Bailey's office as he picks up the phone. He punches the three-digit extension of the Director's secretary.

"Cheryl, I'd like to see the Director. It's rather urgent. . . . Of course. I'll be there."

He hangs up, and begins to calculate his next move.

CHAPTER 18

THAT'S WHAT FRIENDS ARE FOR

Nick Temple sits on his couch again staring at a silent TV. The apartment is still a mess with newspapers, dishes, and dirty glasses strewn about. The doorbell rings.

"It's unlocked," Nick shouts without turning around.

Vanessa Porter enters. Nick's back is to her, but he knows it is her.

"Sorry about the mess. I wasn't expecting company," he lies.

Vanessa takes her overcoat off and hangs it on the coat rack by the door. She walks over and sits down next to him.

"Liar."

Nick shrugs.

"Aren't you going to offer me a drink?

"I think I'll get one for myself while I'm at it. Anyone tailing you?"

Temple gets up and turns off the TV, walks to the kitchen and grabs two clean glasses from a cabinet and the familiar bottle of bourbon from the counter.

"Not really."

"What's that supposed to mean?"

"It's not me they're watching, darling."

"The guys from this morning?"

"The same."

"They're off audio."

"How do you know?"

"I saw the requisition. I still have a few friends inside. You still take it neat?"

"Of course."

Nick pours two drinks, takes a deep breath and picks them up. He walks over to the couch, hands Vanessa a glass and sits down next to her.

"Cheers."

They touch their glasses and take a sip.

"Why am I here?"

"I need your help."

"More help? I thought you might."

"It's all business this time, sweetheart."

Vanessa sets her glass on the coffee table.

"I was afraid of that."

"I think you owe me one."

"Just tell me what you need, Nicky."

"I need to get back in the game. I've got one last chance before they cut me loose for good. You know it's bad when your own men are watching you."

Nick drains his drink.

"You have my complete attention."

CHAPTER 19

SMELLING THE COFFEE

Temple stands behind his desk staring out of his small office window. Richardson and Johnson are in the chairs facing the desk. They are all in their shirtsleeves. Kyle Richardson, steadfast, loyal, a patriot to the core, is stunned. He's not so naïve to think that there aren't a few bad apples here and there, but when confronted with the possibility that someone who is so important to the security of his own country might be selling that country down the drain for a few lousy bucks, his cosmology takes a serious hit.

"There's got to be another explanation."

Bill Johnson feels for his partner. He sees what this might do to his idealism, his drive. But he might as well face it; it's a rotten world.

"Like what?"

"Hush money, the Irish sweepstakes, I don't know. But he can't be mixed up in this."

"Believe it, junior. We've got to keep digging until we find something solid and use it to nail the son of a bitch."

They both look at Nick who continues to stare out the window. Johnson speaks for both of them

"So, Nick, what's the plan?"

Nick is silent for a moment, lost in thought, before Johnson's query settles in.

"What? Oh, right. Let's keep digging."

"Is that it?" Johnson is incredulous.

They all know more digging isn't going to do the trick.

"No. You're right. We need more. If we sit here shuffling paper, by the time we find anything our network in Europe will be so decimated the Soviets will be able to move right in, anywhere they'd like. At this rate, we've got no more than 2 weeks before the damage is permanent. Hell, our sources are already drying up, and I can't say that I blame them. We're not doing such a great job of protecting them. Any ideas, boys?"

Kyle, still somewhat in shock, replies. "I've got nothing. This is out of my league."

"Fresh out here," is Johnson's contribution.

Temple leans forward over the desk, grinning like the Chesire Cat.

"I'm not. I've got the best idea I've had in years. And I was sober when it came to me."

Johnson's not buying. "Sober and alone?"

Johnson is starting to irritate Nick.

"You know, sometimes it feels like I never got a divorce."

'I'm just asking."

"Well don't. . . . Yeah, as a matter of fact, sober and alone."

Richardson gets them back on track. "Let's have it then. Whatever it is, I'm in."

"I'm going in the front door."

Richardson and Johnson stare at him.

"Vasily Malenkov. As far as we know, all that is in the Trade

Mission building is his office, a few interrogation rooms, and some quarters that are supposed to be safe quarters for the agents Vasily runs. Maybe billeting for a few troops. It ain't Fort Knox."

"Why not just walk into KGB headquarters in East Berlin? I'm sure they'd oblige. I'd suggest bringing a revolver, at a minimum. That way you'll be able to shoot yourself before the torture begins." Johnson thinks Nick has lost it, maybe. Or maybe he's got something.

"If we're right that Malenkov is the operational chief on these killings then he's running it out of his office. So, my sarcastic friend, KGB HQ doesn't make any sense."

"Thanks for clearing that up for me."

"We know that KGB lets him run his satellite office because he gets results. I'm willing to bet my ex-wife's alimony check that Vasily's got a file sitting in his office with our traitor's name on it."

Johnson pitches some more sarcasm. "You should phone ahead, let him know you're coming. That way he'll have the file waiting for you."

"Good idea."

Richardson and Johnson look at each other and shake their heads, again.

"No. I mean it; that's a great idea. That arrogant prick will make it easy for me. His arrogance is his weakness."

"Okay, let's say you get in. That's only half the journey, my friend."

Johnson isn't on board yet, but he wants to hear more, to see if Nick has thought this thing out even a bit. Nick sees Johnson is intrigued and thinks it's time to reel the two of them in. He knows Richardson will go for anything that gets clearance from above, so Johnson is crucial.

"That's where you two come in."

"So we're hitched to your coattails?"

"Something like that."

"Another great idea. My career depends on a guy with one foot in the grave. It might not hurt Kyle here, but I've got a family."

"It's the bottom of the ninth, buddy boy. Are you in or out?"

"You know they've got a tail on you?"

"No need for full disclosure then. What's it going to be?"

Johnson looks at Richardson who nods his acquiescence.

"What the hell, right? It's only my career. How about a few details, Nicky boy?"

"That's more like it. Get comfortable, gents. We've got to think this through as thoroughly as we can before I pitch it. I hope you boys don't have lunch plans, or dinner plans for that matter."

"I'll call Peggy. She's gonna chew my ass," Johnson grumbles.

"Kyle?"

"I'm free, Nick. Let's get to it."

Johnson reaches for Nick's desk phone to call his wife and cancel, once again, their dinner plans. Nick opens his desk's top drawer and pulls out a detailed, classified, map of Berlin. The unfolded map covers most of his desk. Richardson comes around to Nick's side of the desk as Johnson finishes dialing.

"Tell her it's for an old friend."

CHAPTER 20

TRUST NO ONE

A man in a black watch cap and navy pea coat walks briskly along a nearly deserted Odessa waterfront in a blanket of fog coming off the Black Sea, the rubber soles of his boots barely giving away his presence; he is virtually invisible. He's an American agent. He and the other agents deep behind the Iron Curtain have received the Soviets' message of the last week. The rules are changing. If you keep at this increasingly dangerous and deadly game, your next breath could easily be your last. Arrest, routine torture, and eventual repatriation through some late night spy exchange across a bridge on the frontier between the capitalist and communist worlds was about the worst he'd feared before the events of the last week. Now anything is possible. He isn't running yet, but neither is he taking any chances.

The mild slap of his boots on the damp concrete produces more noise than he's comfortable with, but there's nothing he can do about it. Less than 100 meters to go to the rendezvous point.

A middle-aged man dressed in work clothes with his head down and the brim of his hat pulled low walks about 50 feet behind the agent. A week ago the agent might have dismissed him; to do so now might be a fatal mistake. He hears the click of a cigarette lighter. Is there a second he hasn't spotted?

The agent picks up his pace before suddenly turning right into an alley, leaning against a building, and pulling out a small pistol. With his free hand he quickly attaches a silencer. Timing is everything. He hears the middle-aged man approaching. Just before he reaches the alley the agent jumps out, puts the pistol against the middle-aged man's chest, and fires twice.

The mortally wounded man clutches his chest and falls to his knees.

As he falls, his eyes wild with terror, he pleads with his assailant, "Pochemu?" He falls flat on his face as the agent strides away, his victim's Russian question "Why?" ringing in his ears.

The agent turns left out of the alley, moving away from the night's rendezvous point, putting some distance between himself and whatever his contact had in mind for him.

"Fuck that," he thinks to himself as he tosses his weapon into the harbor and slowly disappears into the fog.

CHAPTER 21

THE HEAD FAKE

The Director of Central Intelligence looks through a file containing a set of five carefully selected photographs of the meeting between Temple and Vanessa Porter. Cornell Bailey sits across the desk from him trying to gauge the Director's reaction to the photos.

"Did we get any audio?"

"I'm afraid not, sir."

"Damn. What about the paper, anything there?"

"We recovered it. It's an *International Herald Tribune*. Yesterday's edition. Forensics and the crypto boys combed it. Nothing unusual about it. No coded ads, circled words, letters, or numbers. Again, nothing out of the ordinary. We did make some inquiries through our Paris bureau, where the *Tribune's* published. So far as they can determine, there were no unusual requests for that edition. Everything in the paper's on the level. Anything complex would have taken more time than Temple had to sort it out. As you can see from the field notes, he didn't spend more than 15 seconds looking at the paper."

"Did he pick up a copy later?"

"Negative. The paper's a red herring at best, sir."

Bailey wasn't above using the clipped speech of a military officer to make himself sound more imposing, or so he thought. The Director saw it for the affectation it was. It was annoying, but not unheard of from men who envied what a military background did for the careers of competitors.

The Director closes the file; he's closing in on decision mode.

"Is she still in the States?"

"Again, negative. She returned to Berlin on Pan American flight 103, the red eye to London, and then a hop to Berlin. It's all in the report."

"It's too much of a coincidence. Get his financials. If we're going to bring him in, I want it locked up tight before we do. Keep your men on him."

"We're working it in shifts."

"However you want to handle it."

Bailey gets up to leave.

"Will that be all, sir?"

"It's essential that we keep this quiet. If the field finds out there's any hint that the mole's in this office heads will have to roll."

"You'll have to trust my discretion, sir."

"I always do. Temple know we're watching him?"

"I'd count on it. He was good in the field. He may be a bit rusty, but he's not likely to miss something like that. We weren't particularly covert on the photo op."

"All right. Keep me in the loop."

"As always, sir."

Bailey nods and exits. The Director, waiting until he's certain that his Special Assistant is well out of earshot, pushes a button on his intercom.

"Cheryl, find Temple and tell him I want him in my office. Tell him to bring his two boyfriends with him."

CHAPTER 22

SEAL OF APPROVAL

Nick Temple finds himself sitting in a stuffed chair in the Director's luxuriously appointed office; Johnson and Richardson sit on the leather couch against the far wall. The Director sits in another stuffed chair next to Nick. A fireplace with a low-level wood fire burning adds to the feel of a downtown gentlemen's club, an unmistakable sign of success and power. The Director and Temple drink coffee, which the Director finds unsatisfactory under the circumstances.

"I need something stronger. Richardson, bottom left drawer."

Richardson gets up, walks over to the Director's desk, opens the bottom left drawer, pulls out a bottle of single-malt scotch, and delivers it to his boss.

"You pour," he tells Richardson.

Richardson pours into the Director's coffee cup.

"Temple?"

"Thank you, sir. Why not? Hair of the dog, eh?"

The Director nods to Richardson and points at Nick's coffee cup. Richardson pours a shot as directed, puts the cap back on the bottle, and replaces it in the Director's desk drawer. He sits back down. The Director gulps down his enhanced coffee.

"You boys hear about Odessa?"

The others look at each other. Nick speaks up for the team.

"No, sir. What about Odessa." Nick is immediately

apprehensive. He can't help wondering what else has been kept from him.

"One of our operatives killed a Russian civilian."

"Bar fight?"

"Thought he was being followed. Everyone's on a hair trigger over there, and it's going to get worse if we don't shut this thing down. Killed the guy and skipped a scheduled rendezvous. We're reassigning him to Argentina for a while. Can't say as I blame him."

"Are we sure it was a civilian?"

"Affirmative. No KGB traffic, only routine militia chatter; a murder investigation."

"Jesus, that's all we need."

"What about the murder investigation?" Johnson asks.

"It's not going to get that far. He's already out of country."

The Director lets the simple fact sink in: the nation they all swore allegiance to has the power to protect one of its members from a murder prosecution that, in the interests of local justice, should be allowed to run its course. They understand what's at stake globally, but that doesn't make an innocent man's death any easier to swallow. These are soldiers, the type of men willing to kill the enemy, and that's where they theoretically draw the line. They each wonder silently if they'd take such an absolutist approach if they'd done the killing.

The Director takes another sip of his enhanced coffee before he breaks the reflective moment.

"Gentlemen, I've approved your plan. This is not going to look good for the three of you, and there's not a damn thing I can do about it.

If I step in, then our boy's going to back off. He's got to buy it. I'll be able to get you two out, but Temple, I can't make any guarantees about you. Not with your track record. In fact, that's what makes you perfect for this job."

"Understood, sir."

"Just so we're clear, you realize we'll cut you loose if this thing goes south."

Nick finishes his coffee-with-supplement.

"That's the way I wrote it up, sir. I don't see any other way. If you need me to sign something to that effect, I'm happy to do it. Whatever you need."

"No. That's not necessary. In fact, the less we commit to paper, the better."

"Agreed."

"More than two years out of the field and behind a desk is a long time," the Director reminds him.

Nick tries to appear nonchalant. "It's like riding a bike. I'll be fine."

The Director stands up signaling the meeting is over. The others follow his lead.

"That's it then. Good luck, gentlemen. By God we've got to get this thing under control. If this doesn't do it, I'm not sure what we're going to do. Hell, if this doesn't do it, it'll be the next Director's problem and I won't be going down alone, got it?"

They all nod and shake the Director's hand. Nick takes a business envelope out of his jacket pocket and hands it to the Director.

"What's this?"

"Something for my kids. You know, worst case scenario. If I make it back, burn it."

Nick's gesture softens the Director's demeanor. "All right, Nick. I'll see to it, but let's hope it doesn't come to that."

"Look for us in the news, sir."

Temple, Richardson, and Johnson leave the office. The Director stares out the window for a moment, walks over to his desk, gets the bottle of scotch back out, grabs a shot glass from the same drawer, pours himself a shot, and throws it back. He sits down at his desk and pushes the intercom button on his phone.

"Cheryl, tell Mr. Bailey to clear his calendar for lunch."

CHAPTER 23

COLLATERAL DAMAGE

Bill Johnson and his petite, 1950s housewife, Peggy, are in the modest bedroom of their suburban Alexandria home. Bill packs a small black flight bag. Peggy sits on the bed. She dabs at the tears that keep forming in spite of her best efforts. They bought the house when it looked like they were finally settling down. The years of almost constant moving, of military and then civilian government housing were behind them, she thought, and they were at long last being allowed to construct a somewhat normal family existence. But for Peggy, this has the feel of the old days, of the secretive trips, the sudden moves, the unpredictable hours, and she struggles to hide her resentment. Bill knows she is worried, and his feeble efforts to reassure her keep falling flat. She senses, as only one who has been down this road too many times can, that this trip is far from routine.

"It's two weeks at the most, maybe just a couple of days."

"I thought these trips were over."

"This one's special, for an old pal, a lot of old pals in fact."

Bill's slip of what could be considered operational information, an OPSEC violation, surprises him. He thinks to himself that he must be getting soft–too much time behind a desk. Maybe this trip is a good thing, like getting back in shape.

"But, Bill, field work?"

Johnson stops packing and sits on the bed next to the mother of his children, his college sweetheart, the only woman he has ever loved. He puts his arm around her, the best a man who is uncomfortable with affection can do at a moment like this.

"It's not like that. It's a one shot deal, and then back to the office in no time."

Peggy cries softly. Bill decides he has to warn her, even though he knows the warning will undoubtedly add to her anxiety.

"Look, Peg, you're going to have to ignore anything you read in the papers. There's going to be a lot of smoke and mirrors, but you've got to ignore it. No press, no lawyers, nothing. I'll be back before you know it. If things heat up, take the kids and stay with your folks until I get back. If you get any contact from the Company, you'll just have to trust that they know what they're doing and go along with whatever comes your way."

The tears flow freely now.

"You promised. You promised we were done with that kind of life."

He hugs her as she cries against his chest.

"One more time, honey. This is the last time. Like I said, it's for a friend." He stops himself before adding that it's not just for a friend. That what he does is for her and their children, too. It's for families just like theirs all across the country. He does it so their dads don't have to. And no one except a handful of men and women will ever know just how much the Bill Johnsons, the Kyle Richardsons, and the Nick Temples of this country do.

CHAPTER 24

EXECUTING THE PLAN–PHASE I

Snow falls at one of the remaining monuments to Hitler's technological ego–Berlin's Tempelhof Airport. Ultra-modern when first opened, it easily serves the bourgeoning commercial traffic of a post-war world thirty years after it went operational. The airport's architecture belies its origins and connects it hauntingly with its Nazi past. The main building was designed to look like an eagle from the air to stroke the twisted ego of a madman. Most who pass through its busy terminal are oblivious to, and no longer reflect on its appalling genesis. Purposely spared by the Allies during the otherwise total destruction of the Nazi system, the airport has ironically become a symbol of liberty, having served as an island of freedom during the clumsy Soviet blockade of Berlin a decade earlier. When Berliners and the rest of the world stop to think about Flughafen Tempelhof in 1958, they think of its role as West Berlin's vital link to the free world during the heroic days of the Berlin Airlift.

A Pan American World Airways Lockheed L-049 Constellation touches down and taxis to a stop as the furious wash from its four props driven by 2,200 horsepower Wright engines gives way to the early winter wind. A stair ramp pulls up to the aircraft, its door opens from the inside, and Nick Temple disembarks anonymously mixing in with the other passengers. He carries a small briefcase looking like any European businessman hoping for opportunities in the former German capital.

Nick breezes past the passengers waiting to claim their bags and makes a beeline for a phone booth at the far end of the spacious main terminal. A restaurant's neon sign buzzes overhead as Nick closes the phone booth's glass door behind him. Anyone trying to listen will have to compete with the crowd's general din and the multi-lingual announcements of departing and arriving flights. But Nick is unnoticed, an ordinary mid-week traveler likely confirming a reservation at one of Berlin's Pensions.

His call is brief. He hangs up, comes out of the booth, and hails a taxi. He leans his head in the open passenger side window.

"Sieben und siebzig Albrechtstrasse," in his impeccable high German.

"Sofort," comes the response from the driver.

Nick gets in and the taxi speeds away headed for 77 Albrecht Street.

CHAPTER 25

GERMANY'S GETTING CROWDED

The Frankfurt Hauptbahnhof, its central train station, is a huge, glass-covered, busy, classic European train station. Announcements of arriving and departing trains echo from the station's loudspeakers competing with the other busy noises of travel and commerce. Several trains sit at boarding platforms. Newspaper stands, small cafes, a flower store, a sandwich shop/delicatessen, a travel agency, and other assorted shops catering to travelers line the walls opposite the trains.

At precisely 16 minutes before 11 o'clock in the morning, GMT +1, Kyle Richardson, all business, strides through the heavy glass and brass doors of the main entrance into the crowded station. He carries a large black leather flight bag. Without stopping, he looks up at an overhead departure/arrival board indicating which trains are leaving from which tracks. The departure side of the board lists 20 different trains leaving within the next hour for various European destinations. The top entry on the board indicates a train will leave from track 12 at 10:45 a.m. for Berlin, precisely as reported by the Frankfurt station chief to the team when they were carefully constructing the individual missions of their detailed plan on the other side of the Atlantic.

Without pausing, Richardson glances at his Agency issue Bulova Sunburst watch. His timing is exact, and he is grateful for the well-known precision of German rail travel. Also as planned, he has less than a minute to get to the train. Time spent waiting for the train is time spent drawing attention.

Richardson heads for track 12 where the train for Berlin is waiting. Passengers board the train, some in a hurry. Richardson takes a quick look around to see if he is being followed. He jumps aboard just as the train's shrill whistle indicates departure and the train slowly pulls out of the station.

He disappears inside a second class car having spent less than a minute inside the train station. Flawless execution of a simple, but crucial, detail.

CHAPTER 26

JOHNSON JOINS THE FUN

Like its counterpart in Frankfurt, the Bremen train station is a classic, and Bill Johnson has no trouble anonymously navigating his way through the weekday crowd. Johnson carries a large flight bag as he walks towards a train, barely pausing to look up at the departure board. The train to Berlin leaves from track 17 in less than a minute. Johnson follows the same routine as Richardson. No one had to remind them, to instruct them, to tell them that timing is everything. Their approach as they put together their plan was a combination of practice, training, and instinct. Yes, instinct. Even the best training, the most extensive rehearsal can't compensate if an agent's instincts are even slightly off. The Company's job is to cull the best from the best, to identify the agents who will bring that instinct to bear at times when other men would be mentally reviewing a checklist until a bullet or an ice pick takes advantage of the slightest delay and ends their thinking for good. Bill Johnson is one of the Company's best, and although he's had little field work of late, his ability to get himself virtually unnoticed to the Bremen Hauptbahnhof reassures him he'll be fine no matter what this mission may throw at him.

Johnson checks his watch again and heads for track 17. He walks alongside the train briefly to ensure that the car he has picked is destined for Berlin. He waits for the whistle and the first slow movement from the train. He slightly increases the speed of his gait. The car moves alongside him as his foot speed equals that of the train, and without a skip, in perfect synchronization with the train, he steps aboard and into the car, the whole maneuver taking less than ten seconds.

The train gains speed as it leaves the protected platform and heads into the vast rail yard, its mechanical array of steel rails freshly cooled by the season's first significant snowfall. Its most important passenger this morning is Bill Johnson, American CIA agent, who methodically, relentlessly eyes his target.

CHAPTER 27

THE SMEAR

The Director and Cornell Bailey sit in the Director's office. The mood is grim, fatal even. The network they and their predecessors so carefully constructed seems to be approaching a state of total collapse, and now it appears as if the collapse was being orchestrated right under their noses. It's a disgrace that will certainly cost them both their jobs before the week is out. Hell, they might never work again if they don't get the upper hand on what is turning into the single biggest disaster, the greatest failure in clandestine intelligence since the start of the Cold War. It won't be long before the usual jackals up on Capitol Hill start circling, demanding answers, threatening budgets, and selecting heads to roll.

The Director drums his fingers and speaks up.

"Well, this is a helluva note. Are you sure you told them 8:30?"

Bailey's response is, as always, careful, measured, calculated. He is a survivor, and the unfolding drama at Central Intelligence has the potential to test that ability like it's never before been tested.

"Absolutely, sir. It's the last thing we talked about on Friday afternoon."

"What about the tail?"

"No movement out of his apartment since night before last. Either he's holed up in there or he slipped our men."

"Damn it! Why wasn't I informed?"

The Director, furious at the gap in his working knowledge, slams the button on his intercom.

"Cheryl, let me know right away if we get any word on Temple, Johnson, or Richardson."

He lets go of the button without waiting for an answer. The Director looks up at Bailey wondering what Bailey's move will be when the wolves start circling. Bailey's personal loyalty to the Director is what has carried him this far in the Company, but the Director knows Bailey's ability to dodge a bullet, and he doubts that Bailey will simply go down with him. Will he find a new patron, or will he try to fill the vacuum?

"I doubt they're in church, sir. There is the news about the Porter woman."

Bailey's coyness irritates the Director.

"Well let's have it."

"It was in the written briefing. The one with the photos."

The Director knows Bailey is covering his own ass, that his bureaucratic instincts are working at full tilt. He doesn't blame him, but it is nonetheless annoying.

"Well, since you're sitting right in front of me, why don't you tell me in person?"

"She didn't go straight to the airport."

"Damn it, Cornell, quit being coy. Let's have it!"

"She spent about an hour in Temple's apartment, sir." Bailey senses this news is the coup de grâce, a fact that is deeply satisfying given his personal dislike of Temple.

The Director explodes.

"And why the hell am I just finding out about this?"

"As I said, it was in the daily written briefing, sir. I assumed you saw it when we went over the photos."

Bailey remains calm as the Director collects himself and sits silently for a moment.

"Cornell, either there's been a terrible accident or we just found out who our traitors are."

"Game, set, match!" Bailey thinks to himself.

"I'm afraid it's probably the latter, sir. It's the most plausible explanation at this point."

"I can't say that I disagree with you."

The Director needs to keep Bailey on damage control. If he doesn't, he knows his Special Assistant will spend the next 48 hours focused on just how Cornell Bailey is going to come out of this mess. Idle hands are indeed the Devil's workshop. He knows Bailey will relish the opportunity to order others about, to appear as if he, and only he, can carry out the wishes of the Director of Central Intelligence, all of which works in the Director's favor.

"I want you to take charge of this. Make sure their offices are cleaned out. Anything at all that might tell us what they're up to. Their homes, too. Don't overlook a thing."

Bailey knew this was coming and is undeterred.

"I'll take care of it, sir."

"I want a briefing at least twice a day, an oral briefing. If it's in writing, don't assume I've read it, damn it. No matter where you are in the process, call this office. Cheryl will put you through. You have the complete authority of this office. If anyone gives you any static, you send them to me."

For just a moment, the two men stare across the Director's desk at each other, each wondering how the other will survive the week's undoubtedly unpleasant events. Bailey, anxious to appear united against the newly discovered traitors, practically jumps up from his seat.

"We'll get through this, sir. We've been in tougher scrapes than this one."

"Have we?"

Bailey leaves the Director's question unanswered, and it hangs in the room more threat than inquiry.

CHAPTER 28

NOWHERE TO HIDE

At the direction of Special Assistant Bailey, and with near silent efficiency, the Company's tentacles reach out and into the lives of Temple, Johnson and Richardson. Every scrap of paper, every photograph, every keepsake that might provide some sort of clue as to why these three men–patriots in war and in peace who regularly put their lives on the line for their country and their countrymen–might suddenly decide to take up with a despised enemy determined to bring the free world under brutal totalitarian control.

Half a dozen agents in shirtsleeves rummage through the offices of each of the three. This initial foray is broad in scope; they bring out boxes and boxes of items that likely have no intelligence value–family photos, trophies, desk pen sets. Nothing is left to chance. If a clue is in there, the Company's best and brightest will find it. Better too broad of a search that takes more time to evaluate than too narrow of a search that misses the one key that may unlock the bizarre, unfolding mystery of this mass defection. In less than an hour, all three offices are cleared, and their contents are being sorted, catalogued, and examined by a quickly assembled team of the Company's top analysts. If the traitors have left a clue, it will be found.

While the offices are being cleaned out, three separate crews of agents simultaneously hit the homes of each of the men. Temple's apartment is the easiest. No one is disturbed by the ransacking the agents conduct. A few curious neighbors dare peek out at the activity, but in this era of fear of annihilation through nuclear holocaust they know better than to get too nosy about an obviously official intrusion into their mysterious neighbor's life.

The Johnson home is more problematic, and the Company is at least sensitive enough to be aware of the enormity of the intrusion into the lives of an agent's family the search represents. An unmarked, black sedan takes the Johnson family to a nondescript local motel on the outskirts of Alexandria. There they will spend the night, courtesy of Uncle Sam, while strangers go over their most precious personal possessions with fine tooth combs. When they return, they will notice little out of place. An item or two may be missing, but the teams have been trained to make their intrusion nearly undetectable to the civilian eye. The skills that have been used against foreign targets for years will be employed against the family members of three seemingly disgraced men. This, then, is what Bill Johnson warned his wife about; the sudden and thorough intrusion into her family's private life tests her trust and love for her husband like it's never before been tested.

CHAPTER 29

HITTING THE FAN

The Director is on the phone. Cornell Bailey sits on the couch trying to evaluate a conversation while able to hear only one side. He has been in this position before, and he is remarkably adept at filling in the blanks. At least this time, with the President of the United States on the other end, Bailey knows that the directives will be largely predictable. Imagining the President's side of this conversation with the Director of Central Intelligence is not particularly challenging given the political constraints under which the President operates. Still, Bailey has to remain alert. Survival at this level is all about nuances, subtleties, a change in tone or emphasis signaling an important shift in attitude that presages a significant change in policy. He is not about to drop his guard.

"That's correct Mr. President. We're in the process of checking all airports, rail stations, bus stations. Frankly, sir, if these men do not want to be found, it is going to be very hard to find them. . . . Their homes too, Mr. President. They're Company families, and they know the burdens that come with the territory. . . . That's unlikely, sir. We'd have seen something in the press or at least have been contacted by the media if a family member left the reservation. . . . Perhaps they can be of some help. . . . Of course, sir. I'll set up the meeting immediately. . . . Thank you, sir."

The Director hangs up the phone and rubs his temples. The days are not going to get any shorter for a while.

"Cornell."

"Yes, sir?

The Director hesitates. Is he pausing for effect, or is he having trouble believing what he's about to order?

"Better start thinking about an extraction team."

"I'll put it together as soon as we confirm a loc, sir."

"Good. Like I said, twice a day, no matter what."

"Yes, sir."

"That's all, Cornell. If you'll excuse me, I have another call to make."

Bailey, without comment, leaves. The Director waits until he is certain his assistant is within hearing range of the intercom on his secretary's desk and picks up the phone. The President's suggestion about conducting a face-to-face with the Soviet Ambassador was more than idle musing on his part; it was as much as an order that our enemy's representative be probed by our nation's chief intelligence officer.

"Cheryl, get me the Soviet Ambassador."

CHAPTER 30

A BUMP IN THE ROAD GETS FLATTENED

Bill Johnson sits in a second class compartment on the train from Bremen to Berlin. He reads the latest issue of *Life* magazine, passing the time as any casual traveler might. The compartment is packed with five other passengers: two U.S. soldiers, a Russian, and two Germans. Their suitcases in the overhead racks add to the closed-in feeling of the cramped compartment.

The Russian, an overweight pensioner in his sixties, smokes. One of the Germans, a young beatnik type, sleeps. The other German, a rail thin woman in her forties, knits nervously, constantly looking up out of the window. All rock slightly to the train's rhythmic motion. The monotony is broken when two Soviet Soldiers stop at the compartment door and open it.

"Ausweis," the senior of the two demands identification from the compartment's passengers, a routine occurrence once trains have entered the Soviet-controlled East Germany.

The beatnik wakes up suddenly. He and the knitting woman exchange nervous glances unsure what fate lies ahead of them, particularly as they travel through the Soviet zone. For years now, Germans have been leaving East Germany, known officially as the German Democratic Republic, which is neither democratic nor a republic, for the freedom of the west, the Federal Republic. Rumors are constantly floating around that the Soviets will end the drain by sealing the borders and the last thing these two, or anyone else from the west wants, is to be behind the Iron Curtain when the gates slam shut.

All of the passengers, even the American soldiers, produce identification as ordered. One by one, the Soviet goes through them. He saves the American civilian's passport for last. Johnson's American passport gives his name as Alfred Mahan alongside a picture of Johnson that is three years old. Various stamps from European countries easily establish his bona fides as travelling business man Alfred Mahan. The Soviet decides to conduct a brief interrogation. Such a display will not only reveal helpful details about this American, but it will also serve to intimidate the others in the compartment, a bit of sport for the bored soldier. It also gives him a chance to show off his passable English. Johnson hopes the soldier did not run across Captain Alfred Mahan, the late 19th century proponent of the use of America's naval power to project influence into Asia, in his studies back in the Soyuz. He knows he should use a different passport, but trying to pass himself off as Alfred Mahan makes the game that much more interesting.

"Why are you traveling to Berlin?"

"I'm going there on business."

"Which business?"

"I sell women's underwear, if you must know. Apparently there is a shortage in Berlin, and I mean to fill it. That's my business, filling women's undergarment orders!"

The soldier scowls and returns Johnson's forged passport to him. The two American soldiers snicker while the Germans in the compartment cower.

The Soviet soldiers leave, sliding the compartment door closed behind them. Johnson wants to return to reading his magazine, but the Russian pensioner is intrigued. He puts out his cigarette and addresses Johnson.

"Women's underwear?"

Johnson ignores him.

"Let's see your samples, eh?"

The knitting woman quickly puts her knitting away, springs up and leaves the compartment. The American soldiers laugh. One of them decides to goad Johnson a bit.

"Come on, mister, how about it?"

"Perhaps if your gender did not otherwise disqualify all of you."

The pensioner becomes suddenly aggressive.

"You've got no samples? You're no salesman. Who are you?"

Johnson goes back to reading about the funeral of Pope Pius XII in *Life*.

"Maybe you will show your samples to the guards."

The pensioner gets up and leaves the compartment. Johnson needs to stop him, but he can't appear alarmed. He instantly formulates a plan. He pauses, folds his magazine and puts it in his jacket pocket, stands up, grabs his flight bag from the overhead rack, and leaves the compartment following the pensioner.

Johnson works his way through the crowded corridor and soon catches up to the pensioner.

"Look, fella, if you really want to see the samples, I'll show you. Let's step into the W.C."

Johnson grabs the Pensioner under the arm and forces him into an empty W.C. at the end of the car. Three small metallic sinks line the wall under a long mirror on one side of the W.C. Two stalls with metal doors painted white sit across a narrow aisle from the sinks. Johnson locks the door to the W.C. behind them.

"What are you doing? Let me out of here. I will call the guards."

Johnson drops the suitcase to the ground.

"Relax, I'm just going to show you some samples."

The vulgar pensioner smiles, rubs his hands together, and licks his lips.

Johnson, seeing he has correctly read his prey, opens one side of the bag, pulls out a woman's brassiere, and hands it with his left hand to the eager pensioner. As the Russian eagerly reaches for the prize, Johnson smashes the pensioner's nose with the palm of his right hand and instantly finishes him off with another fist to the jaw. The force of the second blow pushes the hapless pervert against a stall door. Johnson grabs him under his armpits, flings open the door with his foot, and sits the accidental tourist, unconscious and bleeding from his broken nose, on the toilet.

He returns to his flight bag, pulls out a roll of duct tape, and quickly tapes the unconscious pensioner's fat mouth shut before taping his wrists behind his back. He wraps the brassiere around the pensioner's neck and hooks it to a pipe on the wall to prop up his head. No more than 30 seconds have elapsed since the pensioner reached for the brassiere.

"No charge for the sample," Johnson mutters with disgust.

He shuts the stall door from the outside and breaks the handle with a kick so that the door cannot be easily opened. He checks himself in the mirror, makes sure there is no blood on his hands or clothes, splashes some cold water on his face, picks up his flight bag, unlocks the W.C. door, and exits. As he heads down the corridor an announcement comes over the train's loudspeaker system.

"Ladies and gentlemen, we will be arriving at the Zoologischer Garten station in five minutes."

The timing isn't perfect, but it isn't bad. It could have been far worse. Johnson derives some small satisfaction from demonstrating that his ability to improvise and overcome has not diminished during his time behind a desk. He walks calmly through the cars to get to the end of the train as far from the W.C. as possible.

CHAPTER 31

NICK TAKES THE PLUNGE

A black Mercedes 180D taxi slides to a halt in the thin layer of slush left by two hours of snowfall. There is ample parking in front of a large, nondescript building in the middle of a busy commercial district. The building is three stories high and just as wide; it looks like a solid concrete block from the street. Other than the front door, it has no windows. Stalinist architecture is a stretch. The building seems to have no architectural details at all. The designer's goal was anonymity, but in a perverse twist of fate, the fact that it is so nondescript makes the building stand out, its drab exterior identifying it as readily as the brass plate, no bigger than 2 feet square, to the right of the door that says Советская Торговая Миссия (Soviet Trade Mission) over an engraved hammer and sickle. A Soviet soldier stands guard to the side of the front glass door.

Nick Temple pays his fare, gets out of the cab, and strides quickly up the steps. He speaks to the soldier in flawless Russian.

"Dobrij Den' (Good day)."

The guard, knowing the penalty if he moves, does exactly as he has been trained. He stares straight ahead, unresponsive.

Nick sees a speaker with a button just below the brass plate. He pushes the button, releases it, and waits.

"Identification, please" a female voice from the speaker firmly requests.

Nick, noticing a closed-circuit camera above the door, pulls out his passport, opens it, and displays it for the camera.

"One moment, please."

Nick puts his passport away and, once again, waits. In that moment of waiting Nick is resolute. His mission is clear. Its rationale is unimpeachable. The alternative is unacceptable. He has often pondered the concept of heroism, and nearly always dismissed it as a salve for the unwilling, an idea created not for the heroic, but for those who benefit from heroic acts. He is far more comfortable with the concept of duty. And at this moment in his country's history, his duty could not be clearer.

The door buzzes, opens, and Nick, knowing there is no turning back, knowing that he has reached the failsafe point, that his fellow Americans may never see him alive again, willingly steps into the building, the belly of the Soviet beast.

CHAPTER 32

DON'T JUDGE A BOOK

Nick takes no more than five steps inside and finds himself in a modest reception area. The walls are bare, with the exception of two photographs in frames, side by side, to his right: Lenin and Krushchev, heroes of the Soviet Union. A Russian woman–the receptionist–no older than 25 and physically fit, sits behind a small, plain, waist-high counter. Nick guesses correctly that hers was the voice on the intercom. A Soviet soldier sits next to her. In front of the soldier, behind the counter, are a closed circuit black and white TV screen and a microphone, all details that begin to tell Nick much more than the building's faceless exterior revealed.

"How may I help you?" the receptionist asks in flawless, if heavily accented, English.

"English?" Nick, feigning surprise, sees a harmless chance to flatter and perhaps slightly disarm.

"Of course."

Nick decided when he first began to put this plan together that there was no point in being coy, so he pulls out his wallet, opens it, and shows his CIA identification to the receptionist.

"I wish to speak with Mr. Malenkov."

The receptionist examines the identification and takes the request in stride, as if Nick is the third CIA agent this morning who has walked into this KGB front and asked to speak with Vasily Ivanovitch

Malenkov, the KGB's operational chief for its East Berlin operations.

"May I take your identification with me, Mr. Temple?

"Of course." She takes the identification from him. Normally Nick would have half a dozen passports with six different names on them from six different countries stashed in various parts of his clothing and briefcase, but knowing a search is imminent, he decided to play it straight. One passport, his, will have to do. He slightly taps his breast pocket to assure himself he still has the one.

"Then I will be back in a moment. If you would please give the guard your briefcase and have a seat."

The guard, dulled by the deadening conformity of the Soviet system, seems barely interested in the remarkable events unfolding in front of him. He turns towards Nick and gestures for the briefcase. Nick hands it to him and the soldier puts it behind the counter without even inspecting its contents. Nick shrugs and takes a seat at one of the two leather upholstered chairs to his right, directly under the portraits. An ashtray stand is between the chairs. Temple lights a cigarette if for no other reason than to break the silence, to add some activity to an otherwise remarkably lifeless scene.

The receptionist comes out from behind the counter and walks down a hallway to her right until the corridor dead ends at a security door approximately 25 feet from the reception area. Nick makes a mental note. She stops and punches a set of numbers into a keypad to the right of the door, using her body to block the view of any American CIA agents who happen to be sitting in the reception area. The door buzzes open. She enters and leaves Nick's sight line.

Nick sees his chance and addresses the soldier.

"Gde vash tualet (Where is your bathroom)?"

"Nalevo (To your left)."

"Mozhno (May I)?"

"Konechno (Of course)."

Nick takes a long drag from his cigarette, stands up, and heads for the bathroom, down the same hall the receptionist took to talk to Malenkov. The soldier follows him. The men's room, marked "Herren," is right next to the women's room, marked "Damen." Both are along the left side of the hallway on the reception area side of the security door. He enters the men's room. The soldier follows him. Nick heads for the bathroom's single stall and enters, throwing his cigarette into the toilet.

"Vyi xhotite nablyudat' (You want to watch)?"

"Nyet," the soldier grunts in disgust.

Nick closes the door. He urinates, shakes, tucks, zips, and flushes. As he flushes he reaches up behind the water basin looking for something, but he comes up empty handed. A look of momentary panic comes over his face. He feels behind the water basin again, this time with fierce urgency. He still comes up empty handed. The noise from the flushing toilet stops and Nick has to come out of the stall. Vanessa! What the hell has happened to Vanessa?

CHAPTER 33

FACE TO FACE

Nick and the Soviet soldier exit the men's room and awkwardly, nearly head on, run into the receptionist and the KGB's operational man, Vasily Malenkov. Nick has seen his picture a hundred times, but the pictures fail to communicate the smooth sophistication with which Malenkov carries himself. This ruthless, cold-blooded enemy of the West could easily pass for a charming British baronet spending a quiet day at his private club in the heart of London.

"Mr. Temple. Thank you for your call. We've been expecting you. How may I be of service?"

Malenkov's tone is politely matter of fact, almost nonchalant, and it immediately defuses the effects of their poorly timed encounter. Nick nods slightly to recognize Malenkov.

"Is there some place private we may talk?"

"Of course. Naturally, I must ask that you consent to a search."

Malenkov may be formal and polite, but he would be foolish to forgo the basics of security.

"Do I have a choice?" Nick decides to apply the slightest pressure to see how it is received. Malenkov is nonplussed.

"You can be searched or walk out of here at once. You should satisfy yourself on that point."

Temple lifts his arms from his side. Malenkov motions to the soldier who thoroughly frisks Temple. He takes Nick's passport out of his jacket pocket, and gives it to Malenkov who inspects it as the search continues.

"Nichego (Nothing)."

Temple puts his arms down.

Malenkov hands Nick's passport back to him.

"I apologize for the necessity of such a clumsy, undignified ceremony. Now, if you will follow me."

Malenkov's insincere apology fools no one. Nick knows that Malenkov would slit his mother's throat atop the Kremlin during the annual May Day parade if he thought such a transaction would improve his political position. Nick works hard to keep his cynical mouth in check while keeping his field agent's brain working at its peak. He's a prisoner who has no more than a few days to escape or perish.

CHAPTER 34

RUSSIAN BALLET

Vasily Malenkov sits at his desk in an office luxurious by Soviet standards. It could be the office of a successful American lawyer. Books in various languages pack the built-in bookcase that lines the wall behind his desk from the top of his room-length credenza to the ceiling. A small serving table with an empty samovar and a tea service sits to Nick's left just past the end of Malenkov's enormous cherry wood desk. The obligatory framed portraits of Lenin and Krushchev together with a huge, lacquered map of the Soviet Union and its satellite nations adorn the oak-paneled wall over the office's door. A series of photos of Malenkov playing polo, a collection of family photos, some generic Russian diplomas, and framed photographs of sailboats to Nick's right complete the picture. The heavy wool drapes are drawn on the floor-to-ceiling windows to Temple's left. Nick concludes that when the drapes are open Malenkov must have a lovely view of a dark, narrow East Berlin alley given that there are no windows visible from the street.

Temple sits in one of two comfortable leather chairs in front of Malenkov's desk. Malenkov takes a cigarette from a silver cigarette box on his desk, and lights it with a similar silver cigarette lighter.

"Forgive me. Where are my manners? Would you care for a cigarette?"

Nick declines, but Malenkov sees an opportunity to boast and to send a subtle warning to the American agent.

"Don't worry. They're not those hideous Russian cigarettes. They're Turkish–a gift from a colleague who recently returned from a business trip to Istanbul."

Nick again declines, but the casual allusion to the Istanbul murder, accompanied by a sly half-smile, instantly confirms his team's suspicions about Malenkov's central role in the recent unraveling. The arrogant prick can't help himself! At least Nick's come to the right place.

Malenkov notices his guest is looking at the lighter. His dealings in the black market are an open secret among his supporters and his adversaries, both in and out of the Soviet Union. His instincts for a rare find have actually served him well all these years in the KGB. His senses are always attuned to a word, a gesture, a hint that would go unnoticed by most. Whether he is trying to secure a Gaugin stolen by the Nazis for his private collection, or he is digging for the identity of the most recent enemy of the state, his eye for the single critical piece of information that will lead him to his goal is usually unerring.

"A relic from another era. One of the few possessions of the Romanovs recovered from their brief stay in Ekaterinburg, before their execution. I won't bore you with how it came to be in my possession, but I must admit, I am quite proud of it."

"Charming," is Nick's response.

"Nothing more than a daily reminder of our past and our struggle for the future."

Nick wants to say, "Why not keep a pile of bodies in the corner?" Instead, in deference to his own survival, he merely states the obvious. "It's exquisite."

"Perhaps a cup of coffee? Do you share your fellow Americans' fondness for coffee?"

"I do."

Malenkov buzzes his secretary on the intercom.

"Svetlana, would you bring us some coffee?"

Nick decides to probe a bit.

"Soviet Trade Mission?"

"A transparent ruse, I admit, but it gives me a certain degree of autonomy, and for that I am grateful. Indeed, the moniker may be appropriate in any case, correct?"

"Perhaps we each have something to trade."

Malenkov turns around, opens a long drawer in his credenza and pulls out a thick file. He places the file on his desk, opens it, and begins to read. As he reads, Nick surmises the file he is looking for is located in the same credenza. Malenkov is just too sure of himself.

"Let's see. Nicholas Harris Temple. Born November 22, 1917. Harvard, class of '39. Studied history and classic languages. Enlisted December 8, 1941, recruited by the OSS, trained in Russian and German. Spent much of the war in London until D-Day. Charter member of the CIA, and except for brief stints on Crete and in Tehran, has been working the Eastern European theater ever since. Married, divorced due to an unfortunate indiscretion, with two children in private school he couldn't afford even before the divorce, all of which has put him deeply in debt. One brother recently deceased–leukemia–perhaps a result of exposure to radiation from atomic blasts during his time in the Army. Should I go on?"

"No need to. I know the story. I just don't know how it ends."

"Which brings us to today, or at least the next chapter. Why are you here, Mr. Temple?"

"I'm here to raid your offices and find out what you know about American intelligence in Europe."

Malenkov laughs politely, continuing his pose as nothing more than an urbane host.

"Well, congratulations! Here you are already in the office of the KGB's operations officer without firing a shot. You'll forgive me if I don't simply hand over my keys to you. Where would the sport be in that?"

"Actually, I'm here to defect."

Malenkov becomes instantly serious. He puts Temple's file back in the credenza. He takes a long drag from his cigarette, puts it out, folds his hands in front of him on his desk, leaning forward on his elbows. His posture and attitude are gravely serious.

"I am a patient man, Mr. Temple, and I am certain that you have a similar file on me back in D.C. that tells you that I am not given to, shall we say, recreational violence. However, I am also a busy man, so I will ask you one more time before I have you arrested and shipped to Moscow, a process you are unlikely to survive. Why do I find myself talking to you this morning?"

"I wouldn't dream of wasting your time or mine. For reasons that will remain mine for now, I am here to defect to the Soviet Union, to place myself and my considerable knowledge of America's clandestine intelligence gathering capabilities and assets at your disposal."

Nick starts to reach into the breast pocket of his suit coat.

"I warn you, Mr. Temple."

Temple pulls back his jacket to expose the pocket. He pulls out his passport, the top of which is just visible above the top of the pocket, and tosses it onto Malenkov's desk.

"I am at your mercy."

Malenkov picks up the passport, satisfies himself that it is the one he has already seen, and puts it on top of the credenza behind him.

"Let us say you are my guest."

Malenkov pushes a button on the intercom on his desk.

"Svetlana, get me Moscow."

CHAPTER 35

CUE THE CAVALRY

Bill Johnson steps off the train just as it pulls into the busy Zoologischer Garten train station in West Berlin. Johnson carries his flight bag as he walks briskly through a group of doors leading out to the street. A sign reads "Kurfürstendamm," Berlin's famous boulevard known to the locals as "Ku'damm," above the doors.

As Johnson quickly puts distance between himself and the train that brought him to Berlin, a conductor walks down a corridor of the deserted train peering into each of the compartments to make sure they are empty. He comes to the end of the car and walks into the W.C. He notices the broken handle on one of the stall doors. A muffled voice comes from behind the door. The conductor grabs the top of the metal stall door and begins yanking at it until it opens.

The pensioner, Johnson's victim of moments ago, sits on the toilet with his hands taped behind his back, his mouth taped with duct tape, blood still trickling from his nose, and a brassiere wrapped around his neck. The startled conductor blows his whistle frantically before stepping forward to help the pensioner.

A gaggle of Polizei in their green and brown uniforms rush past the nearly anonymous Bill Johnson into the train station and towards his victim as he calmly hails a taxi that will take him to the rendezvous point. Before he gets into the black taxi, he tosses a small brown bag containing the remnants of his lunch and the forged passport he used on the train into a curbside garbage can.

The cab winds its way through Berlin until it deposits Johnson at the front door of the Hotel Knoblauch, a small, innocuous, four-story Pension on the corner of Friedrichstrasse and Albrechstrasse. The hotel has a single glass door on the ground floor and each level has three windows that look out onto the street. There are no brochures trumpeting its frills because it has none. Its charm, for Johnson, is its location, less than half a block from the Soviet Trade Mission building. Johnson carries his flight bag into the hotel.

Moments later another black taxi, the ubiquitous Mercedes 190D, pulls up to the hotel, this one bringing Kyle Richardson to the rendezvous point. Richardson gets out with his flight bag. The cab driver gets out, pops the trunk and pulls out a large brown suitcase that Richardson did not have with him when he boarded his train. He pays the cab driver, picks up the suitcase and walks into the hotel. That's it. Two agents upon whose shoulders the fate of American intelligence in Eastern Europe for the next ten years sits. They know the mission, and their training allows them to ignore the obvious pressure.

CHAPTER 36

A ROOM WITH A VIEW

Having completed their transatlantic journey, Bill Johnson and Kyle Richardson unpack in a small room on the third floor of the Hotel Knoblauch. Richardson pulls binoculars, a set of headphones, a directional microphone/antenna, a small tripod, and a bulky telephone handset which has two alligator clips dangling from the end of a couple of feet of wire, out of his large suitcase.

Richardson tosses Johnson the binoculars and the telephone handset. Johnson puts the binoculars down and immediately goes to work splicing the handset into the phone line running from the floor below up the corner of the room, and out onto the public line serving the entire block. The clumsy look of the handset is due to the scrambler/encryption device built into the receiver. Johnson and Richardson now have secure landline comms should the need arise.

Richardson pulls a night stand over and places it under the window. He sets up the directional microphone, which he has placed on the small tripod, on the night stand a bit back from the window. He goes to the window and looks out. Nick is less than half a block away in a building that, if he isn't careful, will be his tomb.

"Got the duct tape?"

Johnson gets the roll of duct tape out of his flight bag and tosses it to Richardson.

"A little less than I started with."

"What?"

"I'll tell you later. No big deal."

Richardson shrugs. He tapes the feet of the tripod to the top of the night stand and tests it to make sure it is steady. He then pulls a small radio receiver out of his large suitcase which he sets on the ground next to the night stand. He takes the wire from the directional microphone and plugs it into the back of the receiver before plugging the receiver into one of the room's two outlets. He switches the receiver on providing power to both receiver and mic. He tests them by putting on the headphones. Any sound picked up by the directional mic will be audible to Richardson's left ear, while transmissions picked up by the receiver will be audible in his right hear. Satisfied that mic and receiver are operational, he takes the headphones off.

Without a word between them, the two men move the room's two small armchairs over towards the window. Richardson turns the room's lights out; Johnson trains the binoculars on the Soviet Trade Mission; Richardson dons the headphones and starts systematically scanning bandwidths starting with HF signals. The receiver's lights seem to grow brighter as the evening settles on Berlin.

"Now we wait."

CHAPTER 37

DEADLY HORSE TRADING

The session stretches into the night. Nick decides he has to give Malenkov something, anything, to secure Malenkov's interest at least temporarily and keep himself alive. Forty eight hours ought to do it, but Malenkov's a tough nut, and it's not going to be easy to convince him that Nick means what he says, especially since he doesn't mean what he says.

He sits in one of the leather chairs in Malenkov's office. He hands a pad of paper and a pencil to his virtual jailer.

"That's it. The Hungarian section's organizational chart, together with names and code names. You want more, I need to start hearing some guarantees."

Malenkov studies the chart for a moment before resuming the air of the overly polite host.

"You have had a long journey. We will talk some more in the morning. In the meantime, you should get some sleep."

Malenkov pushes a button on his intercom. A moment later, Nikolai Gregorovich Kropotkin, a large, severe Russian, in civilian clothes and sporting a crew-cut, enters. Nick thinks, correctly, that Kropotkin has the dull look of an executioner.

"Nikolai Gregorovich, take Mr. Temple to his room. It is not much, I am afraid, but the circumstances, you must admit, are a bit unusual."

Nick stands up, and, keeping with the ridiculous mood of formality, slightly bows to his host who is lighting a cigarette with the silver lighter.

"Until the morning, then."

After Temple and Kropotkin leave, Malenkov takes several drags from his cigarette, savors the smoke each time while he absentmindedly inspects the cigarette. He suddenly crushes it, turns and opens a drawer in the credenza behind his desk, picks up a phone inside the drawer and dials.

CHAPTER 38

I'M STILL LISTENING

Sergeant Dan Mayer sits with a group of enlisted men at a bank of receivers in the U.S. Army's 280th ASA Company Intercept Station in West Berlin. All of the men, "radio jocks" to the initiated, wear headphones plugged into receivers, and each receiver has two reel to reel recorders above it. The lights are dim and blinking lights on the receivers at each position, or "poz" as the men call them, tell even the casual observer the receivers are active. The hum of machine-generated white noise is the only sound in the intercept bay.

Mayer, who is all concentration, suddenly reaches up to switch on one of the reel to reel recorders. He hits another button that uses three radio towers scattered around Berlin to triangulate the frequency. KGB in Berlin! He tries to remain calm and continue his mission as his attention returns to what he is hearing. He grabs the pencil and pad of paper to his left and writes furiously as he listens. He stops writing for a moment, pausing to listen. Another shot at triangulation and the other side of the conversation's location is revealed. He writes down the coordinates, starts the other reel-to-reel recorder and rewinds the first tape. When the tape is completely rewound on a 7-inch reel, he pulls the reel off of the recorder.

"Steagal! Steagal, get over here," Mayer commands as he returns to taking hand copy of the startling transmissions.

Private Steagal, eager, jacked up on lousy coffee, and sitting about four positions to Mayer's left, takes off his headphones and runs over to Mayer. Mayer stuffs the reel in an envelope, scribbles frequency, time, and triangulation data on the envelope, and hands the envelope to Steagal.

"Get this down to the scribes, ASAP. I've got to get my hand copy to the S-2. Move!"

The scribes are the linguists who work in the transcription bay. At this hour of the morning, most of them are working their way through tapes of the day's routine signal traffic, trying desperately to stay awake in the process.

"Jarvis! Get over here and sit on these frequencies. I've got to see the S-2."

Spec 4 Chuck Jarvis takes off his headphones, gets up from his poz and heads over to Mayer. Jarvis, who came to Berlin as a Sergeant, is an undisciplined drunk, which explains why after 10 years in the Army he's been busted down from Sergeant twice, the most recent time for good it seems. When he's sober, he's the 280th's best Russian linguist and most experienced radio jock. He's the man Mayer calls on when they've got to get it right on the first pass. Jarvis picks up the headphones, takes Mayer's seat, and begins to listen. Mayer dashes away for the office of the S-2, the company intelligence officer.

The S-2 for the graveyard shift is U.S. Army Captain Stan Scott. Late twenties, trim, all regular Army, he sits at his desk filling out another round of the endless paperwork the Army loves. His mildly wandering attention is interrupted by an urgent knock on his office door.

"Enter."

Mayer enters, almost out of breath, stands at attention in front of the Captain's desk and, as befits a career non-com, salutes his superior officer. Scott's return salute is autonomic.

"Sergeant Mayer reporting, sir."

Scott knows well the reputation Mayer has for being a bit high strung, and it irritates him to think that this interruption is likely meaningless, that it will only serve to keep him from finishing what needs to be done before the morning briefing for the day shift, the careerists known as the day whores.

"Relax, Sergeant. What can I do for you?"

Sergeant Mayer hands the S-2 the hand copy he took while listening to the intercept. Captain Scott reads it carefully. Mayer can tell he's caught the Captain's interest.

"When was this intercepted?"

"You can see my notation in the upper left hand corner, sir. The transmission started about 15 minutes ago."

"Who are these guys? I don't recognize these call signs."

"They were talking in the clear, sir. I did a triangulation on both. The first guy is KGB. Sloppy, and low-level, but definitely KGB. And right here in Berlin. The other guy is stationed in Magdeburg, probably attached to the 3rd Shock Army, sir. My guess is they're friends back in the Soyuz."

"Are you sure he said defector?"

"Absolutely, sir. Perebezhchik. He said it 3 different times. The guy in Magdeburg was impressed. You could tell by his voice. I don't know why they're transmitting in the clear. If Ivan finds out, they're cooked."

"Look, Sergeant, we've been through this before with you. You thought the Sovs were about to close down the corridors to Berlin when they were just closing a few corridors in the barracks to prep them for painting. Remember that?"

"Yes, sir, but this is the real deal, sir. We've really got something here."

Before Mayer can finish the Captain's desk phone rings. He picks it up.

"Captain Scott, duty S-2."

Captain Scott listens to the other end for a moment.

"All right. Thank you, lieutenant."

He hangs up.

"That was Lieutenant Telleson in the transcription bay. They confirmed it. Defector, three separate times. Good job, Sergeant. Put Jarvis on these guys."

"Already done, sir."

"Nice work. Okay, I'll take it from here. Is that all?"

"For now, sir."

"Dismissed."

Sergeant Mayer comes to attention and salutes. The Captain returns his salute. Mayer executes an about face and leaves the office as Scott dials his phone.

"Get me Brigade's duty S-2 on a secure line."

CHAPTER 39

BACK ACROSS THE POND

Natalie Kramer's modern apartment is as still and as quiet as any at 4 a.m. Her spacious bedroom's king size bed is luxuriously appointed, and its silk sheets partially cover her and her bedmate, Cornell Bailey, as they sleep off another raucous rendezvous. Two piles of clothes on either side of the bed speak to the urgency of their night. In the sitting room down the hall, the second of two empty champagne bottles sits in lukewarm water in a silver bucket. The RCA console stereo is silent, the last in a stack of Frank Sinatra albums having played hours ago. A few embers in the fireplace are the only remnants from the night's earlier flames.

The phone on the bedside table next to Bailey rings. He fumbles for the receiver as the shock of being awake pierces his skull.

"Hello," he barely manages to whisper through the night's mental cobwebs.

Bailey sits up, immediately attentive.

"Yes, sir. I'm on my way. We'll talk before your meeting with the Ambassador."

He hangs up. He sits up and swings his legs off the bed and sits on the bed for a moment as Natalie stirs. She brushes her blonde hair off of her face with her hand.

She is in her late twenties. Although she is disheveled from having just woken up, she is strikingly beautiful. Even a decent tumble in the sack after more than her share of champagne does nothing to diminish that beauty. She is naked, but she uses the sheets to cover her breasts and the rest of her five foot ten inch frame.

"Was that the phone?" she asks with an accent that can only be described as generic Eastern European.

"Indeed," Bailey responds as he reaches for his trousers.

His indiscretion both annoys and concerns her.

"You answered my phone? Isn't that just a bit foolish?"

"It was for me. No harm, no foul, as they say."

"What time is it?"

"Just after four."

"Who's calling you here at four in the morning?"

"My wife. She wants to know if I'll be home for breakfast," he says with slight irritation.

Natalie sits bolt upright, having missed his sarcasm.

"You idiot! You gave her my number?"

Bailey is astonished by her apparent stupidity.

"Relax. It was the Director."

The news that the Director of the CIA knows the home phone number of his Special Assistant's mistress does little to settle her agitation.

"That's an improvement?"

Bailey stands up and zips up his pants.

"Do you think you're the only mistress in D.C.?"

Natalie draws her knees up to her chest and pouts for effect.

"Men are pigs."

He ignores the jab and continues to pick his clothes out of the pile and dress.

"Look, I've got to go in. It's probably nothing," he lies. "Go back to sleep. I'll call you from the office."

He sits back down on the bed, his back to her, to put on his socks. She drops the pouting and switches to temptress, cuddling up to him, putting her arms around him as she does.

"When are we going back to Europe? You never take me anywhere anymore."

Bailey turns to kiss her. She backs away, teasing him.

"Soon. Europe, South America, anywhere you want."

She warms back up to him and kisses him deeply before whispering.

"Anywhere?"

"Say the word, Sweetheart, say the word."

She kisses him deeply again pressing her body against his to remind him why he has risked so much.

CHAPTER 40

NO ONE'S UNTOUCHABLE

Cornell Bailey, fresh from a shower and shave in his office's private bathroom, a clean, starched white shirt practically crackling under his navy-blue, pinstriped suit, strides into one of the CIA's numerous document analysis shops. The large, windowless room is completely secure from the outside world. Even at this early hour, more than a dozen analysts are seated around three separate conference tables meticulously poring over documents. Next to the tables are the boxes taken during the searches of the homes and offices of Temple, Johnson, and Richardson, with one man's name and the location of its origin marked on each box. Anything of the slightest significance is copied and catalogued with the information that caught an analyst's eye highlighted for further review by the entire team during debriefing sessions conducted every two hours like clockwork.

One of the analysts, in the ubiquitous white shirt and thin, black tie central to the Company's culture, notices Bailey's officious entrance. Fully aware of the Agency's organizational chart, the analyst stands up to greet him.

"Special Assistant Bailey, can I help you?"

Bailey musters his best in-charge voice and asks, "Are you running this group?"

The analyst is unimpressed. He's a career man who has seen those in management come and go. He knows Bailey has to puff about for the sake of appearances, but its effect is negligible to nil.

"On this shift, sir."

"Anything yet?"

The analyst rubs the back of his neck.

"It's tame stuff. These fellows look like they play it by the book. Nothing yet." He then decides to take a slight jab at the Special Assistant, a probe that may elicit a telling response. "I'll call the Director if we find anything."

"No need to bother him. Call me. I'll get whatever you have to him."

The response tells the analyst Bailey is running interference. But on whose behalf? His own? He mentally files the response away. You never know when something like that might come in handy.

"If you say so, sir."

Bailey realizes his own mistake, but it's too late. He tries to cover with a little bureaucratic aggression.

"Is that a problem?"

"No problem at all." Bailey's terse question/command makes the analyst suspect the Special Assistant may be running interference for himself.

"All right, get back to it."

"Yes, sir."

Bailey strides purposefully out of the room. The document analyst shakes his head, and, after a moment's reflection, returns to his work.

CHAPTER 41

SHADOW BOXING

The Director stands at his desk as the door opens. He is stiff and formal as befits the occasion. His country is counting on him to learn as much as he can from a man whose vast experience in the fine art of speaking forever while saying nothing is second to none on the planet. That man is Alexei Turgenev, the Union of Soviet Socialist Republics' Ambassador to the United States. Turgenev is dressed in a pin-striped, three-piece suit. He carries a hat in one hand and a cane in the other. Both hat and cane are affectations designed to project the air of a British gentleman to anyone who has forgotten what Turgenev in reality is: a ruthless conspirator steeped in three decades of Moscow's deadliest intrigues. He is a large, distinguished looking man, with a full head of wavy, grey hair. Behind his wire-rimmed glasses are piercing blue eyes deeply set in his large, almost rectangular head. Tufts of bushy grey eyebrows complete his resemblance to a malevolent owl. With the exception of the cane and murderous background, he could easily be an international banker.

The Director walks to him and shakes his hand.

"Mr. Ambassador, I want to thank you for coming on such short notice. Please, have a seat. Is there anything I can get you?"

Turgenev sits and takes in the details of the office of this defender of capitalism. He has spent years in the West, and has grown accustomed to the comparative luxury enjoyed by those at the highest levels of the world's most powerful nation. Still, he is intrigued, and he makes a mental note of his surroundings. He has met the Director on two prior occasions, both on the obligatory Embassy Row party circuit.

"No, thank you. I am quite comfortable. Let's save what I believe you call the chit chat. What is it that I can do for you?"

As Turgenev takes a seat, the Director moves to the chair behind his desk.

"Excellent. Perhaps we can help each other."

The Director attempts to measure the effect of his declining to sit next to Turgenev and instead taking a position of host, of power.

"Always a preferable arrangement." Turgenev, the master statesman, reveals nothing.

"Then I will get right to the point. We have reason to believe that an American citizen who, while on vacation in the American Sector of Berlin, has been arrested by the Soviet Union's Internal Security Committee."

"KGB? May I ask how you have come to believe this?"

"You understand that I am not at liberty to say."

"Of course not. I will certainly communicate with Moscow when I return to the embassy. Perhaps we can clear up this matter. A name might help."

"His name is Nick Temple. He is a career employee of our Defense Department."

"In that case I am surprised that I am not talking to the Secretary of Defense."

Bullshit, the Director thinks to himself. You know damn well who Nick Temple is. Your murderous fucking government spent about 5 years trying to turn him, and let's not forget the half dozen attempts on his life. Instead of saying what he's thinking, the Director stays within his well-rehearsed confines.

"The President has requested that I lead this effort."

"Forgive the question, but is there any chance that Mr. Temple has met some other fate?"

"That is what I am hoping you can tell me."

Turgenev stands up, signaling an abrupt end to the meeting. The Director, concealing his surprise at the sudden termination, stands as well and comes around from behind his desk to stand next to Turgenev.

"I will see what I can accomplish on your behalf."

"You have my direct number, Mr. Ambassador. Please call me at any time."

"Very well."

They shake hands.

"How are Althea, and your children, Fred and Lucy?"

"All fine, Mr. Ambassador, thank you for asking. And your family?"

"Surviving in this dangerous world."

"Perhaps we can make it a bit less dangerous, for all of our families."

"We can only try."

"Thank you, Mr. Ambassador. I look forward to our next conversation."

The Director opens the door to his office and the Ambassador, with a slight nod, exits. His escort, an Army Colonel, meets him the moment he steps out of the Director's office. After a second, Cornell Bailey enters from a side office.

"Did you hear it all?"

"The son of a bitch is laughing at us."

"Well, he as much as confirmed they have Temple. Notice he didn't ask if there was anything more he could do for me. Once Temple's name was on the table, he practically ran out of here."

"Sir?"

"They don't have the other two, or he would have tried to bring it up. But Temple's with them, now; that much is certain. Good Lord, did anyone see this coming?"

"There'd been talk about a vacation for him since the divorce and his brother's death, but, no sir, this is a complete shock."

"What about the other two? Did he take them with him? Did they defect too? Jesus Christ, Cornell, we have got to get a handle on what is going on? With all of our assets over there, we seem to be blind."

"Many of them have gone to ground in the wake of the terminations. The intercepts mention only a single defector, sir. If Richardson and Johnson have defected, their whereabouts are still unknown."

"We've got to get them back. All at once, or one at a time."

"Sir?"

"And soon. I don't care if we have to shoot our way in there. We have to get Temple back. He can rot in hell once he gets back, but he's going to rot in our hell, on our terms, damn it! Didn't we get anything from the searches we did?"

"I've been in constant contact with the analysts' shop. Richardson's squeaky clean, sir. They found a couple of items that raised an eyebrow in Temple's desk, but nothing out of the ordinary considering what he does. Same story with Johnson. A blank. They're either scrupulously careful, or they haven't defected."

"What's the alternative?"

"They're running their own operation."

"Your best guess?"

"Temple's gone, either arrested or defected, most likely defected, and the other two are trying to get him before the Company does. That's one of the dangers of putting these men in teams–sometimes their loyalty gets pointed in the wrong direction. Temple's the key, and probably our mole."

The Director's phone rings. He pushes a flashing button and picks up the receiver.

"Send him right in."

The Director hangs up the phone. The office door opens. Air Force Colonel Wes Peatman walks in. He is in uniform, his hat tucked under his left upper arm. He is tall and thin, but athletic, and at 35 years old he's young for a full colonel, the result of careful maneuvering through the mysteriously connected web of America's vast intelligence community. He has a file in his hand marked TOP SECRET.

"Have a seat Colonel."

"Thank you, sir."

"What have you got?"

The Colonel opens his file for reference as he briefs the most powerful intelligence official in the world.

"We have some fresh traffic from Moscow, sir. H.Q. for Group of Soviet Forces, Germany, has alerted all FEBA general officers to the defection of quote, an American from the highest levels of the CIA who is now a guest of the KGB in Berlin, close quote. Oddly, the alert contains no directives. We also know from our HUMINT sources behind the curtain that a story announcing the defection will be appearing in tomorrow evening's editions of Pravda and Izvestia, sir."

"Jesus. When does Pravda hit the streets over there?"

"About 9 a.m. tomorrow, our time, sir."

The Director looks to Bailey for assistance.

"You'll need to call a press conference, sir. We need to at least get out there before the press picks up wind of this."

"All right. I'm going to stay with what I told the Ambassador. We'll announce the suspected illegal arrest of a civilian employee of the Defense Department while on a sightseeing trip in Berlin. We'll put the heat back on the Soviets. Better clear that with Defense, Colonel."

"Yes, sir. Anything else?"

"What do you make of the lack of a directive in the alert? Seems unusual."

"It is, sir. But this is an unusual case. Our best guess is that Moscow has no idea how to handle something of this magnitude. There's no playbook for it, and various apparatchiks are likely scrambling trying to figure out how to advance their own positions, or at least minimize their exposure. I'm sure we'll see something soon, likely before Pravda hits the streets. Operating in a vacuum is nothing Soviet commanders relish, and the Kremlin has to appear in control."

"Agreed. Well, we'd better hope the other two don't show up in the meantime. That's all, Colonel."

"Thank you, sir."

"Is the file for me?"

"It's yours if you want it."

The Director motions for Colonel Peatman to put the file on his desk. Once Peatman leaves the office, the Director turns to Bailey.

"At least the intercepts confirm the loc. That's good work by someone in Berlin. We need extraction teams over there ASAP. At least three of them. One outside of Stasi, one outside of KGB, and one outside of Malenkov's satellite office. As long as he's still in Berlin, there's no doubt they're holding him in one of those three locations. No more than two at a time on the street per team. We've got to get Temple out of there."

"I'll put it together, sir."

"I want him alive. We have to know how much he's given away. Make sure each team is clear. Alive, Cornell. He dies before we get to talk to him and we'll be in the dark for years."

"I'll have the teams on a morning hop out of Andrews."

"Good work. I'll personally phone in the requisitions so you won't get any static. Anything you need, you've got it. You let me know."

Bailey heads for the office door.

"I want you in Berlin personally overseeing this mission. Take that hop with the teams. Stay in touch with this office."

"Are you sure, sir? It's been a while since I've been in the field."

"You'll be fine. Your instincts are still good. I'd go myself, but, believe it or not, Europe's not the only problem we've got. Take 12 men, three locations, two shifts of two. Pick Berlin vets. You're an old Berlin hand yourself. That's why I need you there. You'll need a good comms man. He's got to be fluent in German and Russian. Stay out of the low frequencies, and use encryption when you . . ."

"Sir. I can handle it."

"Okay. Sure. Sorry. Stay in close contact. I want to know the minute you have anything concrete. I'll let U.S. Mission Headquarters in Berlin know you're coming. They can give you space to run the operation from there."

"You'll excuse me then, sir. I've got some work to do."

"Good luck."

Bailey leaves briskly, all business, trying not to betray his elation. He is certain the meeting couldn't have gone better if he'd scripted it himself.

The Director sits at his desk, picks up his phone, and dials.

"I want to know the quietest and quickest way into Berlin. Meet me in my office tomorrow at 8 a.m."

CHAPTER 42

BOTH ENDS AGAINST THE MIDDLE

Vanessa Porter sits in her fashionable West Berlin apartment, smoking a cigarette, and holding a recent edition of *Der Spiegel* with an ominous warning about Communist China on its cover. The artwork and furniture reflect a mid-century sensibility that is both minimalist and abstract. An original Calder mobile moves slowly with the room's slight current of air. Her legs are tucked under her as she sits on a Gio Ponti designed sofa, typical of her preference for sleek, Italian design, and flips through the magazine paying no attention to any of the stories. Instead, her mind is fixated on what might happen over the next two to three days.

Perhaps she should never have taken his call. A favor for an old friend, and before she knew it she was right back in the thick of a familiar, deadly game. In spite of her state of agitation, she also knows she has missed the adrenaline rush of being a key player in a geopolitical game of the highest order. As dangerous as stepping back into the cloak and dagger world of Cold War espionage is, she relishes it. She needs a break from being the mildly intriguing mistress of this or that thick-waisted businessman willing to shower her with gifts. Nick's call, while it may yet signal her doom, has temporarily restored her to the thrill of life.

The phone rings. She puts out her cigarette, unclips her right earring, and picks up the receiver.

"Porter, hier."

"Vanessa, it's Vasily."

Malenkov's voice is cool, relaxed as always. It triggers a flood of memories of their brief, tumultuous affair. She knew this call was coming, but the timing is off. "Is Nick slipping?" she asks herself. She plays it safe.

"Why are you calling me here?"

"Never mind that. I need to talk to you. It's about our mutual friend. Meet me in half an hour, in front of Kranzler's am Ku'damm."

Without waiting for an answer, Malenkov hangs up. Vanessa stares at the receiver for a moment. She hangs up, picks the receiver back up, and dials a number she memorized years ago. She waits as the phone rings, calculating the time difference between West Berlin and the east coast of the United States.

A male voice cuts in. "Mr. Temple's office. How may I help you?"

Vanessa's face betrays alarm. She immediately hangs up. She knows they'll have recorded her number on the other end, but she had to risk it. Her thoughts turn quickly to her friend.

"Nicky, you are too early," she says quietly as she stands up to prepare herself for her pending rendezvous.

CHAPTER 43

A TASTE OF SOVIET HOSPITALITY

Kropotkin leads Nick down a second floor corridor of the Soviet Trade Mission building. Temple makes a mental note of distances, number of doors, steps to the stairwell, number of stairs, any detail he might need later. The details are all instantly memorized as he calls on years of training and experience, knowing his survival during the next 48 hours will certainly depend on what he has retained from years paid for in blood, sweat and tears.

Kropotkin stops at a door guarded by a lone Soviet soldier. The thick, steel door has a small, closed aperture at eye-level. All appearances belie the ruse that he is a "guest" of the glorious Union of Soviet Socialist Republics. Not yet, at any rate, and maybe never.

Kropotkin opens the door. The room's single light, a bare light bulb dangling by its wire from the ceiling, is already on.

Nick peeks inside. "Who's your interior decorator?"

Kropotkin ignores the wisecrack, motions for Temple to enter, and follows him in.

The room is no bigger than 6 feet by 10 feet with white-washed concrete walls. With the two men in the room, it is instantly crowded. A bed, not much bigger than a cot and consisting of a steel, spring frame and mattress, a lacquered wooden chair in one corner, a sink with a small mirror above it, and a toilet are the room's only amenities.

Kropotkin, clearly disgusted by Temple's existence, offers, "Is not much, but is more than traitor deserves. If you try to leave, you will be shot. Make no mistake."

Temple has seen Kropotkin's type before: a true believer in love with destroying anything contrary to his narrow world view. His experience tells him that men like Kropotkin are tough to kill. They keep coming at you no matter what you throw at them. They internalize the story of Rasputin's death as a personal challenge. Just this side of invulnerable, they refuse to die long past the point that ordinary men would have gone down. Or, as Nick thought more succinctly, this guy is one tough nut.

"I'm not sure your master would approve"

Kropotkin laughs and sneers. He looks ready to spit on Temple if given the chance, to strangle him if given the order.

"Don't be fool! Those are his orders. Do yourself favor. Try to escape. I personally will dump your flabby body into River Spree. It is more than treasonous dog like you deserves."

Kropotkin leaves, shutting and locking the door behind him. Nick notices there is no door handle on his side, another sign that his guest status is a weak charade. The eye-level aperture in the door slides open, and for a second the guard peers in at the curiosity, this western defector, before quickly slamming the small door shut. In spite of the late hour, Nick doubts that his long day is over. The only thing for him to do while locked in this cell is to rest his mind and body for whatever lies ahead of him.

CHAPTER 44

SPIES IN THE COLD

Vanessa Porter paces on the sidewalk near the entrance to the Café Kranzler located in the heart of West Berlin on the Ku'Damm. A few late-night patrons sip coffee and hot chocolate just inside the glass façade underneath the landmark red and white awnings. She is dressed against the cold, her face all but obscured by her high mink collar and winter fur hat. She glances at her watch, a gold, 1945 Girard-Perregaux, to see if she is late. As she gazes up again at the busy street, the firm grip of Vasily Malenkov grips her elbow. How did she not see him coming? Her confidence is briefly shaken. She reminds herself that Malenkov's skills are second to none on his side of the Iron Curtain. The reminder only reinforces her amateur status and heightens her fear.

"Walk with me," he says quietly, threateningly.

They begin walking briskly up the Ku'Damm.

"What has happened to Temple?" Vanessa ventures.

"What makes you think that's what this is about?"

"After you called, I rang his direct line. Someone else answered. That's never happened before. Besides, darling, how many mutual friends do we have?"

"Too many, I'm afraid. Don't worry, your Nick is safe."

"How do you know?"

"He is currently a guest of the Soviet Union."

Vanessa stops dead in her tracks. Malenkov does not try to move her.

"What?"

"Yes. Your American hero defected this afternoon. At least that's what he wants us to believe. Keep walking."

Vanessa resumes walking with Malenkov in tow.

"Do you believe him?"

"It's almost believable. A divorce, mountains of debt, two children in private school. You know, he blames the Army for his brother's death. Then there's that brief business with you. Not so good for his career even if it did keep him in shape for a bit."

"Don't be coarse, Vasily. It's unbecoming."

"If he came to me to trade secrets for dollars, I would have no trouble believing him. But, defection, that is something else. I'm not sure. My colleagues are, shall we say, establishing the bona fides of his claim right now."

Vanessa fights against an image of Nick being tortured by some hero of the Soviet Union.

"This is how you treat your guests?"

"Uninvited guests."

"With typical Russian subtlety, I'm sure."

"Not at all. As you know we are very skilled at extracting reliable information. We should know by tomorrow whether your Mr. Temple is a fraud. If he is, you should shop for a new black dress and a veil. You'll need them both."

She looks him in the eyes as they continue walking and asks, "Vasily, why are you telling me all of this? You know he hasn't been my

Mr. Temple, as you say, for some time now."

"I'm not telling you. I'm warning you. I assumed you already knew. At any rate, if this is all a fraud and you try to help him, it will not go well for you. You can't count on me, no matter what's gone between us."

Vanessa looks away.

"A romantic, Vasily? It's not like you."

"A realist. Remember, you cannot count on me."

"Except to do what is best for Vasily Malenov?"

"What is best for the Soviet Union."

"Oh, stop it, Vasily. I'm not wearing a wire, so please drop the party line."

Malenkov doesn't risk a response. They stop walking. He signals and a black sedan, a Russian Volga, pulls up to the curb. Malenkov's personal driver reaches back and opens the passenger door. Malenkov gets in and the Volga speeds off. Vanessa stands on the sidewalk staring after the departing sedan. In spite of her warm attire and the flush she feels from their brisk walk, a shiver crawls up her spine.

CHAPTER 45

A LATE NIGHT VISIT

Nick Temple sleeps on the small bed in his room in the Soviet Trade Mission building. The door bursts open. Nick is instantly awake and reaches reflexively for a Berretta on a nightstand. Neither are there. Nick's mind clears the moment Kropotkin storms in and turns on the light.

"On your feet, dog."

As two soldiers stand guard, Kropotkin grabs Temple's clothes off the back of the lone chair and tosses them at Nick.

"Get dressed. You have appointment."

Temple stands up and begins to get dressed. He does so slowly, deliberately, infuriating Kropotkin. His pants are on, and as he reaches for his undershirt, Kropotkin strikes him across the jaw with the back of his hand. Temple stumbles and sits back onto the bed.

"Faster, treasonous pig! Faster!"

So far Kropotkin hasn't done anything that even remotely approximates the hell Nick went through during his O.S.S. training years ago. So long as this is all Kropotkin's going to dish out, Nick can take it, but he's fairly certain things are about to get ramped up a bit. He stands up and continues dressing at the same, slow pace. Kropotkin strikes him again.

"Do you not understand your own fucking language?"

"Look, the more you hit me, the longer this is going to take."

Temple has managed to put on his pants and his undershirt, and has just picked up his shirt from the bed.

"That's enough. Go!"

As Nick continues to put on his shirt, Kropotkin grabs his upper right arm and pushes him barefoot out the door.

"You're about to tell us truth, you treasonous piece of filth. You'll cry like wounded bitch and then you'll tell me everything. I bet Svetlana 100 American dollars that I'll have you begging me to stop in under 30 minutes. Ha! Easy money! You'll piss yourself before that, coward. I'll see to it."

"American dollars? Does your boss know you're trading in the black market?"

"Silence, son of Mongolian bitch!"

If there was any doubt in Nick's mind that Kropotkin will throw everything he has at him, it's gone. The door to Nick's cell slams shut behind them. The echo competes with the footsteps of this late night parade, Kropotkin leading the way and the two soldiers three feet behind Nick. The corridor is cold and dark. Kropotkin is right at home, and Nick knows it's going to be one hell of a long night. One night of Kropotkin, he can take; two nights, that'll be a stretch. But three nights? It'll never come to that, and he puts the possibility as far out of his mind as he can. He knows he has to compartmentalize what he's about to undergo, he has to endure each minute, each second, as it comes. If at any point during his pending interrogation he lets his mind wander to what the next second, minute, hour, or, God forbid, day surely holds for him, he just might break. His duty is clear; breaking is out of the question.

CHAPTER 46

NICK AT HIS LIMITS

Nick Temple is in a windowless chamber about twice the size of his quarters. The ubiquitous single light bulb, apparently the apex of Soviet interior design, dangles from the ceiling. The walls are the ugliest, and undoubtedly the cheapest, lime green color the KGB could find. When Nick and his hosts first walked in, Nick noted the familiar lighting scheme.

"I love what you've done with the place. What is it with you tight-fisted commies? Jesus Christ. Spend a few rubles on some light bulbs."

That comment precipitated the first of many blows. And more than two hours later, long after Kropotkin has lost his bet to Svetlana, the hits keep coming. The poorly-ventilated room is dank with the smell of sweat and blood. The acrid odors of raw electricity and burning flesh add to the stench. Only the heartiest of souls could bear to stay in that room for more than a moment. The wretched surroundings no longer register with Nick.

Kropotkin and his two assistants are startled by Temple's endurance, but they know they can outlast him. They've cracked tougher cases before. Men who grew up under Stalin, for whom pain is a way of life, eventually gave Kropotkin everything he wanted. This bloated, spoiled capitalist will do the same, of that they are certain.

In one corner of the room, a large reel to reel recorder is

switched on. A wire runs from the reel to reel connecting the recorder to a microphone hanging from a hook next to the dangling light bulb. Temple, his tattered clothes soaked with blood, water, and perspiration, is strapped into a wooden chair just under the microphone. His chest has several burn marks on it; his face is bruised, cut, and bleeding. He slumps forward in the chair, barely conscious.

Kropotkin motions to one of his assistants and points to Temple's feet. The assistant understands immediately and moves efficiently as he attaches a set of insulated electric cables to each of Nick's big toes via large copper clips at the ends of the cables. He has done this job before, and that's all it is to him–a job. To Kropotkin, it's oxygen.

The attached cables run from Nick's feet to a large black metallic box on a table next to his torturer-in-chief. The box has a thick black electrical cord running from its right side to an outlet in the wall, a small toggle switch on its left side, and a large dial on the front that allows Kropotkin to adjust the amps flowing into Nick's body. Kropotkin nods to the other assistant who pulls a water-soaked sponge out of a bucket and douses Temple's head with it.

"One more time. What are you doing here?"

The beatings have taken their toll, and Nick's voice is barely audible.

"I defect," he says for what must be the fiftieth time in the last two hours.

"Lying garbage!"

Kropotkin toggles the switch and cranks the dial. The lone light bulb dims and Temple goes rigid as the current races through him. His gurgling screams bring a cruel smile to Kropotkin's hardened face. Before Nick stops screaming, Kropotkin turns off the current. He leans over the limp body of Nick Temple and whispers.

"You can't take much more of this, my friend. Why don't you just tell me? I can end all of your pain instantly. Just tell me why you are here. Don't you want pain to stop? Only you can make pain stop."

Temple manages to lift his head just enough to look Kropotkin in the eye. He grins slightly through his swollen lips and eyes and, mustering nearly every ounce of remaining strength, spits a bloody gob of mucus on Kropotkin's face, followed by a weak, yet defiant, "Go fuck your mother."

Kropotkin is instantly enraged, not only by the disgusting spit he has to wipe from his face, but by the prospect of failure, of having to report that his normally foolproof methods yielded nothing more than Malenkov's effeminate interview.

"Filthy, son of whore!"

He toggles the switch again. Temple goes rigid, but his screams are weaker two hours into the ordeal. The jolt lasts for almost five seconds. As Temple screams, as Kropotkin smiles and rubs his hands together with glee, Malenkov bursts into the room.

"Fool! Turn it off! Do it now!"

Kropotkin, jerked out of his reverie by the intrusion, hesitates.

"Why do you wait? Do it now!"

Kropotkin turns off the current. Temple goes silent and limp. The two assistants stand off to the side, waiting to see what is in store for

Kropotkin, hoping to avoid any fallout if it does not go well for him.

Malenkov shoves Kropotkin out of the way and begins to undo the straps holding Temple down.

"Help me free him!"

As Malenkov speaks, Kropotkin motions to the two assistants, and together they undo the buckles and leather straps around Nick's chest, arms and legs.

Malenkov officiously instructs the assistants, all but ignoring Kropotkin's presence.

"Get him cleaned up and put him back in his quarters. He'd better be alive when I check him in the morning."

The assistants, groveling now, convinced they'll be sent to the Gulag should Temple die, gently help him stand. With little strength left in his body, Nick has trouble standing even while being supported under his arms by two of his torturers. He wills himself into a more upright posture. Malenkov leans in and whispers.

"Rest now. We will talk later, without all this savagery."

Temple, unable to move otherwise, weakly nods his head.

Malenkov motions to the assistants and they start to remove Temple from the room, his feet dragging as they struggle to get him out. Kropotkin, seemingly crestfallen, follows them out until he is abruptly summoned back by Malenkov.

"Kropotkin!"

Kropotkin turns and comes back into the room. Malenkov waits until the assistants and Nick are well beyond hearing range before he continues. And when he does, all pretense of rage at Nick's treatment is gone. He and Kropotkin are once again co-conspirators. Malenkov closes the door and puts his arm around his useful thug.

"The chart he gave me is good, if a bit dated. What did he say?"

Kropotkin drops the pose of the chastised bully and begins the routine of cleaning up the chamber as he reports.

"Either he has a will of iron, or he is actually a defector. I took him as far as I could without killing him and he didn't break."

"Okay. Good work. I'll talk to him in the morning. Get some rest when you're done cleaning up."

Kropotkin nods, continues cleaning, and thinks to himself that rest is for the weak, a category he is beginning to move his immediate superior into.

CHAPTER 47

REINFORCMENTS

Cornell Bailey sits at his desk in Washington, D.C. He and the team he has spent the day organizing will be leaving for Berlin in the morning. He has left no detail to chance. He is on the phone, and all business, in full-on Special Assistant to the Director of Central Intelligence mode.

"No excuses. We leave tomorrow at zero seven hundred hours on a hop to Ramstein. We'll catch another hop from Ramstein to Berlin. I'll meet you at Andrews."

He hangs up the phone and stares out the window behind him. He pours a shot of bourbon into a highball glass from a decanter sitting on his credenza. He sips the shot once, holds the glass for a moment, and then tosses the whole thing back before turning back around to his desk.

He picks the phone's receiver back up, dials, and waits as it rings in the West Berlin studio apartment of Karl Schuler. The apartment is small, plain, and neat, to the point of sterility. As the phone rings, Schuler sits on his bed in the process of reassembling a large sniper rifle with a scope, a Russian Mosin/Nagant Ma891/30 with a Zeiss PU scope. Schuler's weapon of choice, whose history is well-known to assassins around the world, is respectfully referred to as "The Victor of Stalingrad" for the key role it played in the hands of Soviet snipers during the winter of 1942-1943. It is one of three he owns and relies on to ply his trade.

Schuler is in his mid-20s, tall and muscular, but lean. He is dressed in dark working trousers and a black turtleneck. His blonde hair is close-cropped, his blue eyes, clear and penetrating. Had he been born ten years earlier, he likely would have been a poster child for Hitler's insane racial theories. As it was, he managed to survive being pressed into service as one of the last pathetic defenders of Berlin during the spring of 1945, before he turned twelve.

He carefully sets the parts of the dismantled, cleaned, and meticulously inspected rifle on his bed before he picks up the ringing phone.

"Schuler, hier."

On the other end is Cornell Bailey, and in spite of the poor transatlantic connection, Schuler recognizes the voice without its owner betraying his identification.

"I have an immediate job for you. I'll send it by encrypted wire. Stand by."

"What's the pay?"

"Double the usual."

"From what I hear you must be desperate."

Schuler picks up and inspects the barrel of the rifle while holding the telephone against his ear with his shoulder.

"You'll see in the wire. I'll need confirmation."

"Triple the usual or shop somewhere else."

"I need a guarantee. The asset must be terminated in Berlin."

"Guarantee? You talk as if you're shopping for a new car."

Schuler puts the barrel down and picks up the high-powered Zeiss scope for inspection.

"Damn it! I don't have time for small talk. Do you want the job or not?"

Schuler gently sets the scope on the bed.

"Same account. There's plenty of room. If you don't receive confirmation within the hour then you'll have to shop somewhere else."

"You're a son of a bitch."

Schuler laughs. "I work for one! So what, we are all sons of bitches."

Schuler hangs up the receiver and picks up the rifle's stock, admiring its fine lines and flawless, sturdy, deadly engineering.

Back in Washington, D.C., Cornell Bailey slams down the phone, takes a deep breath, stands up and strides out of his office, wiping the perspiration from his brow with a handkerchief as he leaves.

CHAPTER 48

THE FOUR-POINT STALL

The CIA's press briefing room is about half the size of the average grammar school classroom. Add in the fact that one fourth of it is taken up by a small stage with a podium, and what's left is room for about 20 folding chairs in four rows of five. That's usually about 15 more chairs than are required. The daily press briefing is opaque and generally meaningless, and the vets of the D.C. press corps stay away. The only attendees are rookies sent out by local papers from Maryland and Virginia, and a conspiracy theorist who managed to get ahold of some press credentials a number of years ago. The CIA lets him attend the briefings. If they didn't, he'd have one more ridiculous conspiracy theory to weave and fulminate about. Besides, the daily briefing is usually an exercise in filling up half an hour each morning with absolutely nothing.

But this evening is different. A Cold War breeze is settling in from Europe, and the press knows it. The fact that the Director of Central Intelligence will be conducting the briefing instead of some GS-13 erases any thought that this one is routine. As a result, the place is packed to overflowing, and the buzz that accompanies the unraveling of a major foreign policy screw up is palpable.

The Director enters a door from behind and to the left of the small stage and strides resolutely to the podium. He is well aware of the need to appear absolutely in control. By the time he reaches the podium the room is deferentially silent, a tribute to the Director's vital importance to the nation's security.

He pulls out a single sheet of paper folded length wise from the breast pocket of his jacket and begins.

"Ladies and gentlemen, thank you for coming this morning. I have a brief announcement to read and then I'll take a couple of questions."

Knowing this is not the moment to extemporize, he looks down at his prepared statement so that it comes across to the press and to governments around the world, including his own, exactly as intended.

"An American citizen, a civilian employee of the Department of Defense, has been detained by the Soviet authorities in the Soviet sector of Berlin. The American Ambassador to Germany in Bonn, working with the Allied Control Council in Berlin, is attempting to ascertain the location and disposition of our fellow citizen. Once those facts have been established, this office will transfer authority for the disposition of the matter to the Department of State."

The Director looks up from the statement while the reporters sit in silence for a moment before erupting into a sea of raised hands and shouts of "Mr. Director!" The Director points to one of the reporters in the front row.

"How about a name?"

Typical rude jerk, the Director thinks to himself. Here's a guy who probably makes six grand a year writing garbage he knows almost nothing about shouting at him as if he were the president of the local school board. He reminds himself that this is the way the game is played, that in a functioning democracy the fourth estate has to puff itself up every now and then in the hopes of being taken seriously. The target just happens to be him today, and he accepts that.

"Sorry. We're going to respect the privacy of his family. We will not be releasing a name at this time." Or at any other time, asshole, he thinks to himself.

The reporters raise their hands again and start shouting again. The Director points to another reporter.

"Is there anything to the rumor that the civilian is actually employed by your office?"

"None whatsoever. This office has been asked to look into the matter given, shall we say, the unique nature of our assets."

A few chuckles, more shouting and hand raising. The Director points to another reporter.

"What about reports that Pravda is carrying a story confirming that the arrestee is actually a CIA employee and that he has defected?"

The Director sees his chance for a disarming exit line.

"If you're getting your news from Pravda then you're in deep trouble, my friend."

The room erupts in laughter, and the Director uses the moment to get off the stage if not out of the spotlight.

"That's all. Thank you ladies and gentlemen. I'll update you when I can."

The Director, knowing full well that most of what he said was a complete fabrication, leaves the stage by the side door at the front of the room. Before he is three steps away from the podium, the reporters begin a mad scramble to get to the bank of telephones in the hall outside of the briefing room.

CHAPTER 49

NOT SUCH SWEET SORROW

Cornell Bailey sits on a black leather sofa in the stylishly appointed living room of Natalie Kramer's apartment, a bourbon on the rocks in his hand. The furniture is sleek and modern for the late 1950s. The walls are sparsely adorned with a few pieces of abstract art. The RCA console is silent; the champagne bucket has been put away by the housekeeper; the fireplace is empty and cold. All is in order. Natalie, in a nightgown next to him, drinks a martini and smokes.

Bailey's news that he has to leave in the morning for business in Europe evokes a predictable self-serving pout from his bored mistress.

"And what do I do while you are off chasing spies? Maybe I'll give your wife a call. We could go shopping. We could swap stories over lunch."

Knowing the last thing on Natalie's mind is killing the goose currently laying golden eggs, Bailey refuses to rise to the bait.

"Wait for me. I'll call you after the dust settles."

Natalie drains her drink, takes a drag on her cigarette, and decides to pour it on.

"Cornell, how many times have you told me to wait? Do you think I'm stupid?"

As she challenges him, she notes with some curiosity that she has never developed a silly pet name for him. The detail briefly, and silently, amuses her. She puts her empty martini glass on the sleek, low-slung, stainless steel coffee table in front of her and continues to smoke.

Bailey takes her free hand in his and tries to placate her.

"This is it. I'm going to tie up a few loose ends and then I'll have enough for us to disappear forever."

Rather than placating her, Bailey's awkward display of affection irritates her. She pulls her hand away.

"I don't want to disappear. I spend half my time hiding as it is."

Bailey grows impatient. He has far too much on his mind to successfully navigate this silly spat with his self-centered mistress. He tries honesty, but the effort is clumsy owing at least as much to his unfamiliarity with the tactic as anything else.

"Natalie, dear, I have risked everything for this moment. The set-up is perfect, and no one will suspect until you and I have slipped away once and for all."

"Maybe it is you who will be the loose end tied up over there."

Bailey drains his drink.

"Don't talk like that. If nothing else, it's bad luck, dammit."

Natalie has heard enough. The evening is going nowhere. She can see he's distracted and she's frankly relieved. Feigning a headache and putting up with his petulant disappointment was not how she wanted to spend the evening.

"You should go."

Bailey, without protest, stands to leave.

"Will you be here when I call?"

As she considers her response, she takes a long drag on her cigarette before putting it out. She wants to see if he'll plead with her.

"We'll see when the time comes."

Bailey, far from pleading, turns and storms out the door.

Natalie sits on the couch, smoking. Disgusted with herself, she quickly wipes a tear from her cheek.

CHAPTER 50

FAILSAFE

An Air Force C-133 Cargomaster, flown in from the 39th Military Airlift Squadron at Dover Air Force Base in Delaware, sits with its vertical stabilizer no more than 10 yards from the entrance to an unmarked hangar on the tarmac of Andrews. Bailey, on the Director's authority, had the massive cargo plane requisitioned for the Berlin job. The plane's four Pratt & Whitney T34-P-9W turboprops are turning, its rear cargo door is open, and its pilot waits for the order to taxi onto the runway for takeoff in the early November morning. This is an "EYES ONLY" mission: the pilot and co-pilot are the only crew members from the Air Force. The navigator, engineer, radio man, load master, and the crew chief are all CIA.

A hangar door opens just wide enough to allow three black Volkswagen panel vans to exit. The loadmaster quickly directs the vans into the cargo compartment of the plane. The vans contain the communications equipment, weapons, and men for the extraction mission. Additional surveillance vehicles are waiting at Berlin Brigade HQ. In all, 12 agents, one communications man, and Cornell Bailey board the Cargomaster in the vans. Loading takes no more than 90 seconds.

Once the last van is in and secure, the cargo door closes, the load master signals the flight deck, the four engines accelerate, and the plane taxis towards the runway, cleared for immediate takeoff.

As the Cargomaster turns onto the runway, the roar of its engines at full throttle signals takeoff is imminent. The plane rolls quickly down the runway, lifts into the early morning air, and with Washington, D.C., off to its left, climbs and banks sharply right to project America's clandestine might half a world away.

CHAPTER 51

POST-OP RECOVERY SOVIET STYLE

The single light in Nick Temple's cramped quarters is on. Nick lies naked on his bed. In spite of the pain from his recent ordeal, he has managed to stay asleep for more than four hours. His face is swollen and cut, his chest a patchwork of burns and scabs. His tattered, bloody shirt is in a heap on the floor. His soaked pants are next to the shirt.

Vasily Malenkov enters quietly. Nick stirs, but is not startled. Malenkov carries a bundle of clean clothes. A soldier behind him carries a tray with hot coffee and a breakfast plate on it. Malenkov directs the soldier to place the tray on the chair and to remove the pile of clothes Nick wore while Kropotkin tortured him. Nick sits up with difficulty, clutching his ribs as he rises. Once the soldier has left, Malenkov sets the clean clothes on the foot of Temple's bed.

"Kropotkin is a pig. He had no authority to do what he did. He was supposed to simply interrogate you. He got carried away and for that I apologize."

"Interrogate?"

Talking is painful at first. Nick flexes and moves his jaw to assure himself that it isn't broken. He stretches and flexes the rest of the body and discovers has no broken bones. That fact amazes him.

"Those were his instructions."

"Something must have gotten lost in translation."

"At any rate, that unpleasantness is over. Have some hot food. I brought you some clean clothes. I don't know if they'll fit. I don't have an eye for these sort of things. Eat, get dressed, and then perhaps we'll have a chat, without Kropotkin."

"I get it. Good commie, bad commie, right?"

"Excuse me?"

"Never mind. How about a bath or a shower? Any chance of that?"

"After our conversation. One thing at a time. Wash up in the sink. The water should be sufficiently warm."

"You spoil me."

"Imagine your treatment if we were convinced that this is all a charade."

Nick decides to go on the offensive.

"Look, you want anything else from me, you keep that goon Kropotkin the hell away from me."

"I'll speak to him, of course."

Malenkov backs towards the door.

"Half an hour then. I'll have the guard come for you." Malenkov pauses for effect. "And Nick, if I may refer to you as your friends do, we'll need more. If you want to stay as a guest, we'll need more. My superiors want me to simply arrest you. I'm not sure they're wrong. Perhaps we'll find out at our next meeting?"

Malenkov bows slightly and exits closing the door behind him.

Temple stands up, still naked, and makes an effort to wash up in the sink. He looks in the mirror at his bruised and swollen face. He is sore all over, but again relieved to know that nothing is broken. If he needs to swing into action, he'll simply have to ignore the pain; at least everything seems to be functioning. Sleeping helped; food will help more.

When he is done washing as thoroughly as he can in the small sink, he dresses gingerly. He puts on every piece of clothing Malenkov left for him. At this point, they are all he has in the world, and he sees no point in leaving anything behind. The grey, dated suit fits loosely. He looks like some low level party member in any one of hundreds of pictures of Moscow's May Day parade he's had the pleasure to analyze.

Once dressed, he sits back on his bed, pulling over the chair with the tray of food Malenkov left for him. He sips the coffee and begins to eat the bland, small breakfast of plain toast and kasha. He sits in his room, in his cell, with a slightly deeper understanding of what compels people to risk their lives to escape from behind the Iron Curtain.

The door blows open. Kropotkin enters, stops, and, with his fists on his hips, his arms akimbo, stares at Nick.

"Excellent suit. Now you look more like citizen of Soviet Union. Perhaps we will let you defect after all."

Nick silently curses Malenkov for doing nothing about his cruel protégé Kropotkin.

"Make it snappy, Kropotkin. I have a date."

Kropotkin walks over to the bed, leans over, and gets right in Nick's face. He places a large, strong hand on Temple's collarbone and begins to squeeze.

"Is that all you got?"

"You have yet to feel what I've got. I should have broken it last night," he sneers maliciously.

As Kropotkin talks, he squeezes harder. The pain shoots through Temple's already battered body, but he does not flinch.

"Is there a point to this, or are you just looking to get another hard on?"

Kropotkin releases Temple's shoulder and laughs.

"If you are going to live in Soviet Union, you will need to be able to endure more pain than that. Finish your breakfast, coward. Comrade Malenkov sent me to tell you that you will not be meeting today. He is indisposed."

Temple stands up and scrapes the food remaining on the plate into the toilet. He spits in the toilet, and then flushes it.

"You guys need a new chef."

Kropotkin slaps him with the back of his hand, knocking him to the bed.

"You're going to need new set of teeth!"

Kropotkin exits, howling with laughter and slamming the door behind him.

Nick rubs his jaw, stretches, and contemplates his next move.

CHAPTER 52

A QUIET INVASION

On the vast concrete apron at the extreme eastern end of Tempelhof Airport, an area off limits to civilians, the C-133 Cargomaster carrying Cornell Bailey and the CIA's extraction team taxis to a halt. The plane's massive rear cargo door opens immediately. The three black Volkswagen panel vans are disgorged. They speed away as the cargo door closes. In less than two minutes, the Cargomaster is once again secure. It immediately taxis back to the runway where it is cleared for takeoff. Commercial traffic sits and waits momentarily as the morning's flight patterns are briefly rearranged to accommodate the mysterious sortie. The entire operation from touchdown to takeoff has taken less than five minutes. As the C-133 takes off, the pilot notes the time in his flight log. There are no notations in any other flight logs of the sortie's existence. The pilots know they'll be turning over their personal logs when the aircraft is safely in its hangar at Andrews. The Company's guiding principle of "plausible deniability" on the mission has been scrupulously, and successfully, followed.

At the gated entrance to the U.S. Mission in Berlin on Clayallee, a U.S. Army MP, a sergeant, spots a black panel van approaching. The van's tags match those described in the morning briefing. The MP motions to a fellow soldier in the guardhouse to open the gate. Without pausing, the van speeds off the street, past the MP, and onto the grounds of the U.S. Mission, coming to an abrupt halt at a side entrance to the Mission's main building. Three men, the van's driver, CIA communications specialist Dave Lacroix, and Special Assistant to the Director of Central Intelligence Cornell Bailey, exit the van. They are met by three men who come out of the Mission from the side entrance. Pursuant to their instructions sent 24 hours earlier by encrypted voice burst, the three men help the van's passengers remove the bulky communications equipment from the van.

In less than 10 minutes, Lacroix is sitting at a six-foot long bank of fully operational radio transmitters and receivers set on a wall-length desk in a secure room on the second floor of the Mission. The bank includes a screen capable of displaying triangulation coordinates from an uplink to Berlin Brigade's hard patches into three radio towers around the city, the same system employed by the 280th ASA. Three more screens look like hybrid television screen/EKG monitors. They provide precise, real-time visual readouts of voice transmissions at three different band-widths, including transmissions on any frequency side band. A spike on any of the screens indicates active comms. While the receiver records the frequency, Lacroix can dial into the transmission from where he sits. At the push of a button, the spike can also be triangulated through the uplink for location coordinates, while audio detection units in each receiver set recording devices in motion. Lacroix is a pro, one of the agency's best, a World War II vet who remained in Berlin after mustering out of the service to provide communications and signal intercept support for the American and British members of the Allied Control Council, and its successor, the Allied High Command. He sits at his position like a concert pianist. His fluency in German and Russian, and his deep working knowledge of the most sophisticated communication devices U.S. tax dollars can buy make him the perfect choice, if not the only choice, for this operation.

A small table with another chair is in the middle of the room. Bailey, a black flight bag in his hand, motions to the others who have assisted with the set up to leave the room. Lacroix waits for them to leave before speaking to Bailey.

"Perfect. I'll fire it up and we'll do a comms check with the field teams."

Bailey sets his bag on the small table.

"Good. I'll check in with D.C."

Bailey leaves the room while Lacroix puts on a set of headphones with a microphone attached and starts flipping switches on the bank of equipment bringing it, and his mission, to life.

←─ ←→ ←→ ←→ ←→ ←→ ─→

A black 1954 Mercedes sedan with German license plates pulls into a parking spot across the street and slightly north of the Headquarters of the East German Ministry for State Security, the dreaded Stasi. The sedan contains two extraction team members, their weapons, communications equipment, and supplies for the potential extraction. The van they arrived in is in a West Berlin chop shop being reconfigured for the black market. The planned switch in the garage of the motor pool at Andrews Barracks in Lichterfelde was executed without a hitch. Anyone who saw the van arrive at Tempelhof would have found it impossible to locate the van and its contents less than an hour after its arrival.

The team member in the passenger side of the vehicle picks up the push-to-talk mic from the HF radio the team installed.

"Team Alpha in loc 1. Over."

He releases the push-to-talk button on the mic. Dave Lacroix's voice comes on the radio.

"Roger, Alpha."

"Alpha out."

He replaces the mic in its cradle knowing that Lacroix has had sufficient time to triangulate the signal to confirm its genesis. Now they wait.

KGB Satellite Headquarters in East Berlin sits innocuously on Hohenzollerdamm. The giveaway to its existence are areas on either side of the street for 50 meters in front of its main entrance. These are carefully guarded zones in which no unauthorized automobile is allowed to park or even stop for any longer than it takes for an armed guard to order removal.

A beige Mercedes 220S with German license plates pulls onto Hohenzollerdamm. As prearranged, a taxicab pulls out of a parking spot 80 meters north of and on the other side of the street from the KGB's front entrance just as the Mercedes pulls into view. The sedan immediately occupies the vacated parking spot.

The team member in the passenger side of the vehicle picks up the push-to-talk mic from the car's recently installed HF radio.

"Team Bravo in loc 2. Over."

He releases the push-to-talk button on the mic. Dave Lacroix's voice comes over the radio.

"Roger, Bravo."

"Bravo out."

He replaces the mic in its cradle.

The scene is repeated as Team Charlie sits in a 1958 black Opel Rekord in front of the Soviet Trade Mission building. Slightly more than one hour after touchdown, all three extraction teams are seamlessly in place.

As he drew up the plan, Bailey worried about its predictability. As he reviewed it, as he briefed it, he became satisfied with it. Routine is a Soviet trait. In all of his years of working to defeat or at least contain the Russians he'd come to understand their aversion to improvisation. They could do it when push came to shove, Stalingrad had proven that. But Bailey understood that their first instinct is to stick with the tried and true, to go by the book so long as one exists. In his considered judgment, if Temple is still in Berlin, he's in one of the three buildings now being watched by American CIA special operations units under the direct command, for better or worse, of Special Assistant Cornell Bailey.

CHAPTER 53

A NEW NEIGHBOR MOVES IN

Directly across from the U.S. Mission on Clayallee, set 75 meters back from the street to allow for a sidewalk and a greenbelt that will act as the apartment building's yard, a block-long, four story apartment building is under construction. It's the sort of project familiar to Berliners; more than 13 years after the last Allied bombs were dropped on the city, the rebuilding continues. Any time so much construction is happening all at once in the same general locale, the chances for graft and corruption increase exponentially. The Bauleiter, or construction manager, on the Clayallee Apartments project is not immune to taking kickbacks from contractors to ensure their bids are accepted. So long as the quality of the workmanship is high, no one will complain. Such is life when construction is booming. Besides, so much of the money flowing into the former capital is foreign aid from the United States that skimming a bit off the top seems only natural, certainly acceptable, and practically mandatory.

When the Bauleiter was approached 24 hours earlier by Karl Schuler, he was as cooperative as he was surprised. All Schuler asked for was three days of undisturbed access to an incomplete unit nearly in the center of the project on the top floor of the unfinished building facing the street. He was in no mood to ask questions when Schuler not so subtly made it clear that he knew of the Bauleiter's kickback activity (an accurate bluff on Schuler's part confirmed by a stumbling, groveling response) and was willing to go to the American command with his knowledge. What surprised him was that Schuler still offered to pay five thousand American dollars for the access, to which he immediately acquiesced. He thought about contacting the Polizei, but then he'd have to forfeit the $5,000, an enormous sum to receive all at once, even for an honest man. And, of course, what he did not know was that had refused the bribe, had he made any noise at all about the Polizei, the Americans, his superiors, or any other authorities, Schuler would have killed him on the spot. Instead, his hand was open, his mouth was shut, and no one was the worse for it, or so he thought.

Karl Schuler, dressed like a construction worker, crosses the street directly in front of U.S. Mission to the unfinished apartment building. The workday is over, but lights hang here and there partially illuminating the exterior of the construction site. Shuler wears a navy blue watch cap and carries what appears to be a large, canvas bag of tools. He ignores the sign commanding Kein Eintritt–Do Not Enter–and walks by a number of "Vorsicht!" signs advising him to look out for the various hazards he might encounter on this, or any, construction site.

He picks his way through piles of studs and rebar, pallets of cement bags, a variety of cement mixers, and other typical construction site debris until he turns to enter the completed shell of the apartment complex. He crosses into the building through what will soon be a stairwell entrance on the off-street side, but is now simply a framed threshold. He walks quickly, noiselessly, up three flights of unpainted metal stairs. At the top of the stairs he turns into the unfinished apartment selected on a visual inspection shortly before his successful encounter with the Bauleiter. He winds his way through the apartment's unlighted halls, past framed rooms, some of which are already sheetrocked, until he comes to a room with a window frame that looks onto Clayallee. He glances back to make certain his position in the apartment cannot be detected from the entrance. Having satisfied himself on this point, his gaze turns to the front of U.S. Mission Headquarters. He is no more than 10 meters down the street from being directly across from the Mission's gated entrance.

Schuler drops to one knee, unzips his canvas bag, and pulls out a folding stool and a rifle scope. He positions the stool slightly to one side of the window frame so that when he sits on it, he cannot be seen from the street. From his sitting position he looks across the street at the Mission entrance through the scope. The position of the MP guard house on the far side of the entrance gives him a greater range of access to vehicles and pedestrians entering the mission compound from the street. Except for slight movements to the left and right to scan the entire sector, he is perfectly still as he begins the coldly efficient mental process of selecting and sequencing potential targets.

CHAPTER 54

IN THE DUCK BLIND

Kyle Richardson, headphones on, sits at the window of the hotel room he shares with Bill Johnson. He rolls up and down the HF range on the receiver–spinnin' and grinnin' as the SIGINT boys call it–searching for a blip, a word, a piece of a conversation, anything that might provide a picture of what's going on inside the Soviet Trade Mission building just down the street. Bill Johnson sits back from the window and slowly, methodically scans the street with a pair of binoculars. Their mission has the feel of combat guard duty at this point, a duty characterized by long stretches of monotony, pierced now and again by moments of sheer terror.

Johnson sets down the binocs and asks for what seems like the one hundredth time in the last 24 hours, "Anything yet?"

"No. They're still jamming. On top of that, those walls look to be about three feet thick. I doubt we'll get anything unless we get lucky with our land line splice. You?"

"Routine traffic."

Johnson picks the binocs back up and returns to scanning the street for a moment. He stops suddenly.

"That's her."

He sees Vanessa Porter walk up to the front door of the Soviet Trade Mission building. She has a large purse slung over her shoulder.

"You sure it's her?"

Johnson responds without losing his target.

"Absolutely, and she's about 36 hours late if it's her first visit. Our boy could be cooked if she screwed this up."

"Let's see how it plays out."

"Not much choice at this point. Nick might have to improvise."

Neither man had ever had much faith in the part of Nick's plan dependent on Vanessa. Her involvement seemed almost self-indulgent on Nick's part. They suspected he was well aware that her role was the weakest link in the chain of events, and that he'd thought through the need for alternatives from the get go. They were all about to find out.

CHAPTER 55

BETTER LATE THAN NEVER

Vanessa Porter holds her Ausweis–her West German identification card–up to the closed circuit camera at the front of the Soviet Trade Mission. The door buzzes, and she enters realizing that her next move may be fatal. Perhaps not today or even tomorrow, but at some point, deep in the night, she'll likely pay a terrible price for what she is about to do. The simple act of helping a friend is enough of a threat to one of the world's superpowers that it could be the last act of a life that would get mixed reviews at best. She buries her doubts and anxiety as she steps into a role she reminds herself she willingly accepted.

Once inside, Vanessa walks confidently up to the reception area. The same Soviet soldier and receptionist that greeted Nick's arrival are again on duty.

Vanessa removes her gloves and addresses the receptionist in English as she would address the hired help.

"Please tell Vasily Malenkov that Vanessa Porter wishes to see him."

The soldier, unimpressed, barely glances up. The receptionist, however, responds with the polite formality Malenkov requires. That formality includes continuing in English, a language Malenkov actually prefers to his native Russian.

"Of course, madam. One moment, please." Vanessa puts her

gloves in her oversized shoulder bag. The utilitarian bag is oddly out of place given her otherwise fashionable ensemble. It is filled with a ridiculous assortment of cosmetics, combs, handkerchiefs, keys, and other random knick-knacks. At the bottom of the bag is an antique, sterling silver necklace worth well over $2,500.

The receptionist picks up a telephone receiver and presses the first in a row of buttons on the bottom of the phone.

"A Miss Vanessa Porter to see you, sir. . . . Of course, sir."

The receptionist hangs up.

"He will be with you momentarily. May I offer you a cup of coffee, or perhaps a glass of water?"

"Thank you, no. May I use the ladies room while I wait?"

"Of course. Down the hall, to your left. You'll see it."

"Thank you."

"If you would, please leave your bag with me."

Vanessa takes the large bag off her shoulder and hands it to the receptionist. She turns to walk down the hallway, but the receptionist stops her and then motions to the soldier.

"One moment, please."

The soldier comes out from behind the reception desk and faces Vanessa. It is clear he is going to search her.

"For security purposes," the receptionist explains matter-of-factly.

Vanessa shrugs to signal consent. The soldier starts at her shoulders and pats down the outside of her statuesque frame. He squats as he proceeds down her body while the receptionist watches with interest. When he reaches the hem of her skirt, his hands work their way back up the inside of her knees and thighs. Vanessa closes her eyes against the indignity of having this thick-fisted peasant's hands nearing her crotch. He looks up, leers, and breaks off the search just as Vanessa is about to protest. He stands up, and searches her jacket pockets before continuing the body search. He slows down at her breasts, leers again as Vanessa's eyebrows raise in the only form of protest she dares, and finishes where he started, at her shoulders.

Vanessa opens her eyes to see his dull face jerk in the direction of the hallway letting her know she is free to go. The receptionist's half-smile betrays her glee at the weak, decadent westerner's discomfort.

Vanessa turns and walks down the empty hallway and quickly comes to the two restrooms. She glances back to see if the receptionist and soldier are looking. As she hoped, they are busily inspecting the contents of her bag. Vanessa slips silently into the men's room.

Once inside she takes a quick look around and sees no one is in the bathroom. She enters the lone stall but does not close the door. She reaches under her dress. A plastic bag containing a Minox B camera, no bigger than a pack of chewing gum, is taped to the inside of her thigh as high up as she dared put it, less than an inch from where the soldier broke off his search. She grimaces slightly as she rips the bag from the inside of her thigh. She then tapes it to the back of the ceramic water basin above the toilet. She waits a moment before flushing the toilet and leaving. She walks briskly back to the reception area and sits down certain that her watchers, who are just now finishing their inspection of the contents of her bag, did not notice her choice of restrooms.

Before she has time to remember to ask for her belongings to be returned to her, Vasily Malenkov appears.

"Miss Porter. How may I assist you?"

Vasily's detached tone is irritating, and Vanessa is tempted to say, "Oh, knock it off, Vasily, or I'll let your comrades know how much you enjoy a vigorous spanking in a Turkish bathhouse."

Knowing that discretion is the better part of valor, she instead plays the role the moment has assigned to her.

"I need to talk to you about someone I believe is a mutual friend."

Malenkov motions to the receptionist. The receptionist comes out from behind the desk.

"Please hold your arms out from your side."

"Again?" Vanessa asks in protest.

The receptionist frisks Vanessa as thoroughly and with as much obvious pleasure as the guard had moments earlier. Vanessa's eyes narrow as she gives Malenkov a contemptuous glare. He shrugs.

"Nothing," the receptionist reports.

"If I'm to be repeatedly searched, perhaps I should simply take off all my clothes for our meeting."

The receptionist hands Vanessa her bag, undoubtedly lighter by one antique, sterling silver necklace. Malenkov ignores Vanessa's petulance, and directs her towards his office.

"Right this way, Miss Porter."

Vanessa helps herself to a cigarette, lighting it with Malenkov's silver cigarette lighter. She knows its origin–he made sure of such on a previous visit–and how much Malenkov prizes it. As she lights her cigarette, Malenkov half sits, half leans against the edge of his desk facing her. She is fascinated by his uncomfortable attempt to appear informal and at ease. She does not look at him.

"Now, Vanessa, to what do I owe this distinct pleasure?"

She reaches into her bag and pulls out a thin, manila envelope, and hands it to him. The envelope was innocuous enough to have escaped close inspection by the reception personnel. Malenkov takes the envelope, walks around behind his desk, sits down, and opens the envelope with the solid gold letter opener on his desk. He slowly looks over the documents. There are less than a half dozen of them.

"And why are you bringing these to me? What interest do I have in the financial indiscretions of this or any American?"

"It's insurance, Vasily?"

"How so, my dear?"

"Someone is cleaning house over here, and, frankly, I think it is you. But you're being helped. You're paying dearly for it, but you're getting help."

"If any of that were true, what has that to do with these?"

"Don't act as if you're stupid, Vasily. It isn't flattering."

"As usual, you'll have to help me. I don't know what to make of it, and you are so much more clever than I."

"If I'm on your list, Vasily, take me off. If anything happens to me, the originals go straight to the Americans. Copies with instructions are on their way to my solicitor in London."

Malenkov leans forward, a sudden look of malevolence overtaking his face.

"And, my dear, have you considered the effect of your clumsy threat if you are last on my list?"

"If I'm anywhere on the list, you'll have to kill your inside man too. It's all in there. You won't get anyone to work for you for a decade if you do that. You'll be finished, Vasily. You'll spend the rest of your days stamping Pacific fleet shipping invoices in Vladivostok."

Malenkov stands slowly, walks behind Vanessa, and starts to caress her neck. She refuses to face him, remaining calm in spite of knowing he would kill her on the spot if he was convinced she was a threat. She continues to smoke as he speaks.

"There was a time, Vanessa, when our conversations were not quite so business-like." He continues caressing her neck, slowly applying pressure, moving from her neck and shoulders to her throat.

"It was always business, Vasily. And it served us both well." She takes another drag on her cigarette, desperately trying to keep her hands from trembling, wondering if her next breath will be her last.

He begins to tighten his grip on her neck. She can't help looking startled, but she does not move. Suddenly, she is certain he is about to kill her, but just as quickly, he relaxes his grip, and she exhales. He gently strokes her hair.

"You know you wound me when you suggest I would ever harm you, Vanessa."

"I know you, Vasily. You would trade your mother to the Chinese for an Italian suit. And now, I would like to go."

She stands up and he backs away from her chair.

"You are free to go, of course."

She turns and walks past him towards the office door. Before she can get to the door, he speaks up with his back to her.

"Vanessa."

She stops at the door to and turns. He turns around slowly, stops when he is facing her, and remains silent.

"What is it, Vasily? Or are you just going to stand there like some sort of ridiculous statue of Lenin?"

He ignores the insult to his carefully cultivated western appearance.

"Do not overestimate the value of your insurance policy, Vanessa. You have been traveling a good deal lately. Perhaps you should travel some more."

She stares at him for a moment, his thinly-veiled threat ringing in her ears as she turns quickly and leaves.

Malenkov picks up the lighter, walks behind his desk, and lights the documents. He drops the flaming pages into his wastebasket, watching to make sure the conflagration consumes them completely.

CHAPTER 56

WATCHING THE WATCHERS

In the Hotel Knoblauch, Johnson and Richardson fight off the natural urge to settle into a routine. Stakeouts can be mind-numbing, but the agents' mission requires them to remain alert. Immer wachsam, as the Germans say. The fireworks could start at any moment, and when they do, the two men must be able to engage instantly.

Johnson surveys the Trade Mission Building, the street traffic, and the foot traffic for any sign that the status quo has changed or is about to change. Richardson eats a sandwich as he scans the airwaves for relevant chatter. Johnson suddenly announces.

"She's coming out. Mark the time."

Richardson checks his watch and makes a notation on the pad of paper he's been using for intercept hand copy.

Johnson follows her movements to her car with his binoculars. He scans the street and notices Team Charlie's Opel Rekord parked three cars beyond Vanessa.

"Whoa! We've got company. Take a look."

Richardson takes off his headphones as Johnson hands the binoculars to him.

"Three cars back. Check it out."

Richardson fixes on the black Opel momentarily before asking, "What do you make of it? Extra security?"

"No way. Those are our guys."

"Reinforcements?"

"Not a chance. This one's off the books, remember? Just the four of us."

The light bulb clicks on for Richardson. "The Company's put together an extraction team. They're here to grab Nick."

"Exactly. If we play this thing right, they'll do our job for us."

"What if it's a termination mission?"

Richardson's question is legitimate, but without being on the inside, it's impossible to answer. Instead, Johnson remains non-committal.

"We'll see when the time comes. Once Nick gets what he needs, everyone's cards will be on the table. See if you can pick them up. You know the SOP on frequencies, and at the very least they have to do comms checks."

"I'm on it."

They both go back to work as they silently contemplate what effect, if any, the presence of at least two more American agents will have on their ability to pull off what was at best a long shot before this latest wrinkle appeared.

CHAPTER 57

LIFE'S A BITCH AND THEN YOU DIE

Vasily Malenkov has made his decision. Nick Temple will be arrested and sent to the Soviet Union where he will be tried as a spy. Before the day is out, Malenkov has decided, he will set in motion the process that will provide the evidentiary basis for the charge of espionage. Once he receives confirmation that a sufficiently credible case, albeit completely false, has been constructed, he will formally arrest Temple, all to his great credit. He hates to admit it, but Rozenchenko is right: the Americans will do nothing other than bluster. Eisenhower, the great American war hero, has shown his reluctance to engage the Soviet Union over much larger issues. The arrest and prosecution of a CIA agent will barely merit inclusion in a single morning briefing from the President's National Security Advisor.

Then there is the matter of Vanessa. While Malenkov hates to see such beauty and sexual agility extinguished, her death can be used to buttress the case against Temple. The forged documents needed to establish her perfidy are already being prepared. "She has less than 24 hours to live," he thinks gleefully to himself. "Such is the price for having the audacity to threaten me!"

And now he must turn his attention to Temple. He pushes a button on his desktop intercom.

"Bring our American guest to me. And a samovar of tea."

He turns to look out the window of his office as he rubs his hands together. His thoughts turn to the month-long vacation on the Black Sea that will surely be the reward for his handling of this entire affair.

Nick lies on his bed drifting in an out of sleep. The swelling on his face has gone down a bit, but it is still bruised. Scabs have formed over the various cuts. Kropotkin, the source of Nick's physical pain, enters.

"On your feet, coward. Comrade Malenkov wants to see you," Kropotkin barks. Although Kropotkin's tone is unchanged, Nick's failure to crack impressed him. However, for Kropotkin to display even the slightest respect for this enemy of the state is unthinkable. He is resolute.

Temple sits up, swings his legs off the bed, gets up gingerly, and puts on the suit jacket.

"Lead the way."

Kropotkin motions to Temple to go out first. Temple shrugs his shoulders and leads, walking stiffly, all the while working hard to flex and loosen his aching muscles sensing he may soon need them all working at top capacity.

They walk down the hall towards a door at the top of the building's main stairwell. They pass through a security door before coming to the stairwell, and head down two flights of stairs. Temple says nothing that betrays his fear that at any moment a bullet might slam into his skull from Kropotkin's sidearm. Instead, they simply walk past the main reception area and towards the door leading to Malenkov's office. Temple stops at the men's room.

"May I?"

"What is it with capitalists and toilets? How did you ever fight war without being able to find restroom every 30 minutes?"

"Look, if you had gone a little easier on my kidneys maybe I wouldn't have to take a piss quite so often. What the hell is it to you, anyway?"

Kropotkin shakes his head and nods towards the restroom.

"Go. Are you sure you don't need to use woman's room?"

Kropotkin roars with laughter at his own joke as Temple enters the men's room.

He goes immediately to the restroom's only stall. He turns around to make certain Kropotkin has not followed him in. Satisfied that he is alone, he closes the door. He hears Kropotkin pop his head in through the door and yell.

"Bystro, bystro (Quickly, quickly)!"

Temple urinates and then flushes the toilet. While the sound of the toilet covers his movements, he again feels behind the water tank. Jackpot! Vanessa made it. He puts the Minox in the breast pocket of his jacket before quickly reaching behind the water tank again. He finds nothing. "I guess I'm on my own for firepower," he thinks to himself.

The noise from the flushing toilet stops. Temple exits the stall pulling up his zipper. Kropotkin has just entered the bathroom.

"I was about to send in rescue team to drag your worthless, feminine carcass out."

"What the fuck's the hurry, big boy?"

Kropotkin grabs Temple's left bicep and drags him out of the restroom.

"Your new Soviet master awaits."

The two of them head towards the security door in front of Malenkov's office. Temple pauses as Kropotkin punches in the access code. The door opens with a buzz, and Kropotkin pushes Temple through.

"You can find your own way from here."

Kropotkin retreats behind the security door and closes it. Temple straightens out his coat, takes a deep breath, and knocks on Malenkov's door.

"Enter."

Nick opens the door. Malenkov stands behind his desk, his suit jacket unbuttoned, the butt of a pistol in a shoulder holster just visible under his left arm.

"Nick, come in, come in. Please, have a seat."

Nick is sick of Malenkov's feigned charm. He seats himself in a chair in front of the desk. Malenkov comes over to inspect Temple's wounded face.

"Each day you'll look better. Nothing permanent I trust. You are healing nicely."

"Kropotkin's good."

"He is an animal, but a useful animal. I am certain there are such creatures on your side of the so-called Iron Curtain–a stupid phrase. Would you care for some tea? While you Americans prefer coffee, it is tea that a Russian cannot resist. You'll have to learn new habits, eh? A year from now you'll blend in as if you were born in Leningrad."

A samovar is on a small table right next to Temple. Malenkov pours two cups of tea from the steaming samovar. He hands one to Temple. Nick's cup shakes as he brings the piping hot liquid to his lips. He recoils as the tea scalds him.

"Thanks for the burn. Are you guys all sadists?"

Malenkov ignores the insult. He has grown weary of Temple's sarcasm, and thinks about how much he'll relish this insolent prick's torture and execution.

"About the organizational chart you gave me."

"What about it?"

"Simply put, it's dated, and of little use to us."

"It's a helluva lot more than you've given me."

Malenkov lights a cigarette with his silver lighter. He takes a long drag, and walks back over towards Temple, stopping to stand directly on Temple's left.

"You're finding your room and board not to your liking?"

"You're shittin' me, right?"

"Perhaps you should start by telling me what it is you would like."

"I already told you. Call off Kropotkin, for starters."

"Yes, I am sorry about that. Kropotkin again exceeded his orders. He will be punished."

"Bullshit. He'll be given a medal."

Malenkov is beginning to lose his patience.

"Excuse me?"

Nick decides to lay it on.

"I said bullshit. No one in your whole stinking country does anything they're not ordered to. Kropotkin has been following your orders, and you're following someone else's. You're a cold-blooded killer, and all of this gentlemanly bullshit is just that, so you can knock off the act."

Malenkov can no longer hide his agitation. He takes a deep drag from his cigarette, leans over, and exhales directly into Nick's face.

"I assure you, Mr. Temple . . ."

Before he can finish, Nick flings the scalding hot tea into Malenkov's eyes. Malenkov recoils in agony. Nick grabs the silver cigarette lighter from the desk and crashes it into Malenkov's skull. Malenkov crumples to the floor.

"Score one for the Romanovs, asshole."

Nick Temple springs into action. He puts the lighter back on the desk. He then rips the cords from one set of drapes. He turns Malenkov over on his face, quickly tying his hands behind his back. He pulls the cord out from the base of a standing lamp and binds Malenkov's feet together. He then rolls Malenkov over and pulls the handgun, a 9mm Makarov PM, from Malenkov's shoulder holster. He checks to make sure it has a fully loaded clip. He then walks over to the credenza behind Malenkov's desk.

Using the lighter to smash the lock, he opens the drawer and starts rifling through the files. He pulls out a file marked **Корнзлл Байлий**, puts it on the desk, pulls the Minox out of his jacket pocket, scans the Russian documents, and quickly takes 6 pictures of the file's key documents. He rifles through Malenkov's desk drawers, finds four extra 8-round magazines for the Makarov and pockets them.

No more than 60 seconds after being struck by his own sadistic memento, Malenkov begins to stir. Temple walks over to him and kicks him fiercely in the head knocking him out cold again.

"We'll see who heals first, motherfucker."

The intercom on Malenkov's desk buzzes several times. Nick realizes he has only seconds before an armed response will blast through the security door. He bursts out of the office and into the corridor. The door with the keypad opens. The soldier from the reception area sees Temple. He goes for his sidearm, but he is too slow. Temple fires once. The round slams into the soldier's throat, and continues until it slices his spinal cord paralyzing him for the last awful moments of his life.

A piercing klaxon alarm starts to pulsate throughout the building. Nick will have to shoot his way out.

CHAPTER 58

OUT OF THE FRYING PAN

Team Charlie's two extraction team members, Wade Rogers and Perry Cooper, hear the alarm go off in the Soviet Trade Mission building.

"Better call it in," Rogers instructs.

Cooper pulls the push-to-talk mic from the radio.

Dave Lacroix, mic and headphones on and all concentration on what is unfolding, sits at the bank of radio receivers and transmitters in the U.S. Mission. He turns to address Cornell Bailey who is standing over him.

"Sir, an alarm has gone off inside the Trade Mission. Cooper and Rogers want to know if they should go in."

"Give me the headphones."

Lacroix takes the mic and headphone set off and hands it to Bailey.

"This is Special Assistant Bailey. Stay put. The alarm could be anything. No sense giving ourselves away. Stay put."

Lacroix looks at Bailey with astonishment as Bailey hands him back the mic and headphones.

Temple runs down the corridor from Malenkov's office towards the reception desk. The female receptionist fires at him using the desk as cover. He does a summersault into a kneeling position and returns her fire.

The unfolding gun battle is audible from the street.

"That's gunfire. Tell Lacroix we're going in."

Cooper picks up the push-to-talk mic.

"Shots fired. We're going in."

They jump out of Opel, slam the doors and run across the street with the .45 Colt Automatics they selected for this mission drawn.

Bill Johnson looks through binoculars. Kyle Richardson rips off his headphones.

"Gunfire!"

Johnson puts down the binoculars.

"Those boys are going in. We're outta here."

Johnson and Richardson, who are already armed with pistols in shoulder holsters, blow out of the room.

One of the rounds from Temple's furious return fire slams into the top of the receptionist's skull killing her instantly. The hurried footsteps of several soldiers can be heard coming down the stairwell behind the reception area. Temple drops an empty clip from the Makarov and reloads.

Rogers and Cooper bound up the stairs of the Trade Mission with weapons drawn. The Soviet soldier standing guard reaches for his sidearm. Rogers shoots and kills the soldier. Cooper tries to open the door, but it's locked. Both team members take a step back and pump half a dozen rounds each into the glass door, shattering the glass into a thousand pieces. They drop their clips and reload before going in.

Inside, Temple takes cover as the front door shatters from the fusillade. As he turns to shield himself he sees the first of a group of soldiers coming down the stairs. He fires, dropping the first soldier at the base of the stairs.

Rogers and Cooper burst in through the destroyed door. They instantly recognize Temple from the file they studied on the hop to Ramstein. They join him in firing into the stairwell, forcing the other soldiers to retreat as they fire and drag their dying comrade with them. Bullets are ricocheting wildly, but the Americans are as yet unscathed.

"CIA. You're with us Temple, or we'll drop you right here," Rogers yells as the furious gunfire continues.

"Then I guess I'm with you," Nick yells back.

Nick stoops and makes a dash for Rogers and Cooper who unload two more clips into the stairwell. The three of them continue to pour rounds into the building as they back up through the door to the street. They run down the building's front steps, dash across the street, dodging traffic and onlookers, until they reach Team Charlie's car. Rogers gets behind the wheel, Cooper takes shotgun, and Nick dives into the back. They speed away, but they are not alone.

CHAPTER 59

INTO THE FIRE

Kropotkin races through the shattered front door of the Soviet Trade Mission at full tilt and firing. He runs to a Volga parked by the curb directly in front of the building, jumps in, starts the engine, executes an immediate U-turn scattering the daytime traffic, and chases after the extraction team sedan.

A black 1957 Chevy Bel Air, with Richardson at the wheel and Johnson riding shotgun, bolts out of the parking garage next to the Knoblauch Hotel. They accelerate over the 30 feet to the corner of Friedrichstrasse and Albrechtstrasse and, without slowing down, skid through a 90-degree left hand turn just in time to cut off Kropotkin.

Rogers looks in his rearview mirror to see Kropotkin cut off by a speeding, skidding Chevy.

"Jesus, where did those guys come from?"

Cooper leans out the passenger window and fires at the trailing car. The car swerves as its driver evades Cooper's fire, but it loses no ground.

Nick, in the back seat, loads the last of his four spare magazines and turns around to fire at the following car. He sees Richardson and Johnson in the car and shouts, "Stop firing! That's a Chevy, for Christ's sake! Those are our guys."

Cooper continues to fire and shouts, "Our guys? Who the fuck are our guys? I thought you were a defector."

"Is this the face of someone who just defected? And what about the last two minutes? Are you shittin' me? Head east!"

Cooper stops firing.

Rogers, who's driving, asks, "East?"

"The Sovs are going to think we'll run like hell for the American sector. You go east and you'll buy some time while they shift assets around. Then we'll cut back west."

Rogers glances over at Cooper.

"East it is."

"I'm calling it in."

Cooper picks up the radio mic. Rogers cuts the wheel hard and the car speeds and skids through a sharp right turn at the next intersection.

←—←→←→←→←→←→—→

Dave Lacroix has his headphones on. Cornell Bailey continues to hover right behind him. The next several minutes are make or break for Bailey, and he's not leaving anything to chance.

"Team Charlie has him, sir."

"Good work. Stand down the other teams. Tell them to head out to Tempelhof."

"Sir?"

"You heard me."

"Shouldn't they try to meet up with the other team for fire

support? SOP, sir."

"They'll never make it. Besides, I want us to be ready to take off as soon as we have him."

"Yes, sir."

Johnson weaves the Chevy through traffic to keep up with the extraction team sedan. A bullet from Kropotkin obliterates the car's rear window and pierces a hole in the front windshield. Johnson looks in the rearview mirror.

"Jesus, that son of a bitch is getting close."

"Why'd he go east?" Richardson asks as he fires at Kropotkin.

"Switchback. He heads east. Our son-of-a-bitch friend back there radios it in. The Soviets commit resources for the intercept. Then Nick heads west, the resources to stop him aren't in place, and he just might slip through. Didn't you learn anything in Korea?"

"I don't know if you got the memo, but there weren't a whole lot of car chases in that war."

Another bullet passes through the passenger compartment and out the front windshield.

"Jesus!"

Richardson fires back at Kropotkin. He hits Kropotkin's windshield and a headlight, but Kropotkin, who is calling in his position, keeps coming.

Cooper can see Richardson firing at Kropotkin.

"They're not firing at us."

"You believe me now?"

"Look, the Director told us . . ."

"Watch out!"

Rogers cuts the wheel and barely misses a pedestrian. They continue to careen wildly through traffic.

Nick tries to get a shot off at Kropotkin, but the distance combined with both cars' movements makes firing nothing more than a waste of ammunition.

"Where's your second car?"

"What?"

"Come on, we don't have time for this. Standard Agency practice. Where's your second car?"

Cooper relents. "Podbielskialle, just across from the u-bahn."

Nick visualizes a street map of Berlin in his head and announces, "Perfect. Left at the next intersection."

They speed towards the intersection. The light is green for the cross traffic.

Rogers is undeterred.

"Hold on, boys!"

Rogers picks his spot, and cuts the wheel hard to the left sending the car swerving and skidding. He makes it through the intersection without getting hit. He is still followed closely by Richardson and Johnson, with Kropotkin, like a machine, firing relentlessly, and not far behind.

CHAPTER 60

NO VACATION FOR YOU

Russian medics attend to the dead and wounded in what moments earlier was nothing short of a combat zone. A Soviet soldier with a mic and headphone set on sits behind the reception desk now splattered with the blood and skull fragments of the recently terminated receptionist. Her covered, lifeless body lies near the foot of the blood-soaked stairwell. Malenkov, his face badly bruised, is pacing in front of the reception desk. He thinks about making a dash for the street, but he is certain he would be shot before he got to the sidewalk. Kropotkin is his only chance. Kropotkin! The thought of being indebted to Kropotkin is only slightly better than the fate that awaits him if Kropotkin fails.

"Nothing since his last transmission, sir," the soldier reports.

"Are they still heading east?" Malenkov

"I have no idea, sir."

Malenkov goes into a rage.

"Incompetent fool! Call headquarters. Confirm that they have dispatched all available emergency personnel to block all roads headed east. Keep trying to raise Kropotkin."

"Yes, Comrade Malenkov."

"Do it!"

The cleanup continues around Vasily Ivanovitch Malenkov, a man whom the building's survivors already regard as little more than a walking corpse.

CHAPTER 61

TWO IN THE BUSH

"You know the u-bahn station at Wittenbergplatz?" Nick asks Rogers.

"I do."

"That's our next stop. We'll dump the car there, get on the u-bahn and ride it to Podbielskiallee. We'll never shake this guy on the streets. The u-bahn to car number two's our only chance."

"You're the boss."

"When did that happen?" Cooper asks.

"About five minutes ago, or haven't you been paying attention?" is the best Rogers can offer.

The three cars continue their wild and deadly chase through the heart of Berlin. A wake of shaken motorists, downed bicyclists, and cowering pedestrians has attracted the attention of the Polizei. In the distance, Nick and company can hear the wailing approach of their sirens.

Moments later, the black Opel pulls up and stops in the middle of the street in front of the entrance to the Wittenbergplatz u-bahn station. Temple, Rogers and Cooper jump out and run down the stairs from the street to the underground portion of the station and onto the train platform.

Johnson and Richardson see their three fellow Americans abandon their car in the middle of the street.

"Pull over. Maybe we can stop the chase right here."

Richardson slides the Chevy to the curb. They both leap out, ready to fire.

Kropotkin sees the abandoned car. To save time, he simply opens the door of his car while it's still going close to 30 miles per hour and rolls out. The car bounces off of oncoming traffic, jumps the curb, and finally collides with a concrete wall lining the outside of the u-bahn station. The normally hard-boiled, unflappable Berliners transform into terrified pedestrians, shrieking and running for cover.

Like a robot with a laser-like, unrelenting focus, Kropotkin is virtually unscathed from his high-speed roll. He stands up and runs towards the station escalator. Johnson and Richardson open fire on Kropotkin from their car, but they only get a couple of shots off. Kropotkin's left bicep is hit, but the wound does nothing to slow him down.

Johnson and Richardson get back in their car and speed away before the West Berlin Polizei arrive.

Temple, Rogers, and Cooper scramble down the escalator and board the first car of a train sitting at the platform, the train's doors closing right behind them. As the train pulls out, they can see Kropotkin clearing a path down the escalator, flattening terrified civilians on his way to the platform.

Kropotkin is undeterred by the fact that the train is leaving the station as he arrives at the platform. He runs alongside the accelerating subway, and jumps onto the back platform of the last car, just managing to hang on as the train speeds into a tunnel at the end of the platform. He calmly drops his empty clip, reloads and fires three rounds into the glass door of the car. Shattered glass flies into the passenger compartment as Kropotkin reaches in and opens the obliterated door from the inside. He starts methodically working his way through the screaming, cowering crowd towards the car containing his prey.

Johnson makes a sudden turn off Kleiststrasse on Wittenbergplatz. Richardson hangs on through the turn and the ensuing chaos in the intersection before speaking up.

"Where are we going?"

"Clayalle. The U.S. Mission. If Nick gets there, he's safe. It's the closest place that makes sense. Turn on the receiver. See if you can get anything from the other team members. They've got to have a comms guy working the team. I need to get over to Hohenzollerdamm."

Richardson flips on the receiver of the push-to-talk radio in the car as Johnson weaves through traffic.

Kropotkin has nearly worked his way to the front of the train leaving a trail of broken glass and terrified passengers in his wake. He is within two train cars of Temple, Rogers, and Cooper as the train pulls into the Podbielskiallee u-bahn station.

It's midday, and the platform is crowded. Temple, Rogers, and Cooper get off the train and run for an escalator. They bound up the escalator and are soon at street level.

Kropotkin gets off the train and tries to follow, but he is stopped by a uniformed transit officer at the train's door. The clueless officer is conducting a random ticket check. He stops Kropotkin with an outstretched arm.

"Fahrschein, bitte (Ticket, please)."

Kropotkin goes into a rage. He speaks in heavily accented German.

"Ticket? Here is ticket, you son of fascist whores!!"

Kropotkin pumps three quick rounds into the unfortunate transit officer's chest. The crowd screams as Kropotkin bolts for the escalator.

He reaches the street level just in time to see Temple, Rogers and Cooper jump into a beige Mercedes 220S parked across the street from the u-bahn station. The car skids away from the curb. Kropotkin fires to no effect at the fleeing car, oblivious to the thick crowd. Furious, he heads back down into the u-bahn station.

CHAPTER 62

I'VE GOT SOME BAD NEWS, AND SOME BAD NEWS

Back at the Soviet Trade Mission, one of the survivors of the recent bloodbath, the soldier with the mic and headphone set, has been trying without success to raise Kropotkin.

"Chaika, this is Zhurabal, over. Chaika, this is Zhurabal, over. . . . I've got him sir!"

"Give me the headset."

Without waiting, the panicked Malenkov rips the headset out of the soldier's hands. He holds one earphone up to his right ear, and with his other hand holds the mic to his mouth. The soldier notices Malenkov is shaking so badly he can barely hang on to the mic.

"Kropotkin, god dammit, where are you?"

A look of terror comes over Malenkov's face as he listens to Kropotkin's response.

"Wittenbergplatz! That's west!" he screams.

Malenkov listens in stunned silence. The soldier can barely make out another muffled transmission coming out of the headphones. Malenkov, slowly hands the headset back to the soldier.

"What are your orders, Sir?"

Malenkov stares at the floor for a second and then recovers long enough to issue a desperate order that even he knows is destined to fail.

"Radio headquarters. They are to transfer the emergency personnel to roadblocks at the edge of the American sector."

"But sir, they are all east of Frankfurter Allee."

"Issue the order. It is my personal command! Do it!"

Malenkov, nearly blind with rage and fear, paces as the soldier works the radio. Suddenly, the soldier takes off his headphones and stands up.

"What is it? What are you doing, fool? Get back to work. You have your orders!" Malenkov screams.

"KGB headquarters has informed me that operational command has been transferred to their offices and that I am to cease any efforts on your behalf."

Stunned, Malenkov nearly collapses. He braces himself against the bullet-ridden reception desk, and barely able to stand, he makes his way to the chair Nick Temple sat in a mere 48 hours earlier. He collapses into the chair, slouching, robbed finally of all of his energy.

The soldier pulls out his sidearm.

"I have been instructed to confiscate your firearm to prevent you from trying to take your own life."

Malenkov, barely conscious, makes no response. The soldier comes out from behind the desk. With his pistol pointed at Malenkov's temple, he flips back his former boss's jacket to reveal an empty holster. Malenkov recovers sufficiently to address the soldier.

"It's gone. It's all gone. And you're looking at a dead man."

The soldier returns to his post to provide his new superior officer with a situation report as Malenkov stares in shock, knowing his life isn't worth a counterfeit kopek.

CHAPTER 63

THE HOME STRETCH

Rogers, who is at the wheel of car number two, the 220S, is elated.

"Did you see that? Ha! Looks like we made it, buddy boy. You're home free."

"I'll believe it when I'm back in the U.S. He had a radio in his car. If he gets back to it, we're still in the soup. You can't outrun a radio."

Nick grimaces as the pain of his recent beatings, a pain he'd been able to suppress during the adrenaline rush of the escape, once again surfaces.

Cooper turns to Nick and asks, "You gonna make it?"

"Sure. They didn't break anything that I know of. Just their way of saying 'Welcome to the Soviet Union.'"

"Is there a package back there?" Cooper asks.

Nick looks around and sees a brown paper package on the floor.

"You want it?"

"Not yet. Hold tight. I just wanted to make sure it got in the car."

Cooper picks up the push-to-talk mic from the car's radio. He pushes the button on the mic.

"HQ, this is Team Charlie. We're coming in. Over."

Dave Lacroix's voice comes over the radio's receiver.

"Roger, Charlie. What's your loc? Over."

Cooper looks out the window and picks up a street sign.

"Drakestrasse, 1400 block. Over."

"Roger, Charlie. I'm picking up Herm traffic indicating a road block on Siemenstrasse. Get over to Bernauer. It's coming up and it's still clear."

"Bernauer. Roger. Out."

Rogers cranks the wheel and the car takes a sudden, screeching left down Bernauerstrasse.

Johnson and Richardson come to an intersection that is completely blocked. Johnson slams on the brakes to avoid adding to a pile up.

"Christ! We've got to get out of here. Hold on."

Johnson slams the car into reverse and starts weaving his way backwards through oncoming traffic that's getting denser by the moment. He executes a reverse right turn down a side street, does a skidding 180-degree turn, and accelerates down a side street.

"We'll just have to take a detour. Nick's gonna beat us to Clayallee. Not good."

CHAPTER 64

HOW SOON THEY FORGET

Malenkov is on the phone in his office. He has recovered enough to take one last shot at saving his own neck.

The Communist Party political officer, the Zampolit, for Group of Soviet Forces Germany, in the signature black trench coat and black fedora of his rank, sits at Malenkov's desk.

Malenkov slams down the phone.

"Fool!"

He addresses the Zampolit.

"Kropotkin failed. He lost them at Podbielskiallee. He radioed in his failure. It was the only time he radioed in during the entire operation. Complete incompetence."

The Zampolit is unimpressed. There are few in either the KGB or in the Communist Party in Berlin who are not by now aware of the pending fate of Vasily Ivanovitch Malenkov. His name is already being forgotten by those who were his closest colleagues when he woke up that morning. He is an instant leper on the fast track to death and historic oblivion, the blot that ended his career, and all references to Vasily Ivanovitch Malenkov to be systematically purged from all records of the otherwise glorious Soviet Union.

"I would not be too hard on Kropotkin. He is a good soldier. It seems to me the failure is all yours, Comrade Malenkov."

The Zampolit gets up from behind the desk and begins to walk out of the office. He stops and turns, to make certain there is no question about Malenkov's fate.

"Comrade Colonel Roznechenko will be most displeased. We'll have to shut down the operation. Just when it was getting profitable. You will keep yourself available, Comrade Malenkov."

"Of course."

The Zampolit turns and leaves, passing an armed guard posted just outside of Malenkov's office.

Malenkov sits back in his chair and finally breaks down, sobbing like a coward, unable to reconcile himself to his pending fate.

CHAPTER 65

A DEADLY OBSTACLE COURSE

Cooper reports in to Dave Lacroix at the U.S. Mission in Berlin.

"Less than a minute out. Over."

Dave Lacroix responds.

"Roger, Charlie. Out."

Cooper replaces the mic in its cradle and turns to Nick.

"Almost home. Now it's time for that package."

Nick hands him the brown paper package. Cooper rips it open and pulls out a black trench coat identical to the ones he and Rogers are wearing and hands it to Nick.

"Put that on."

Temple takes off the hideous jacket he got from Malenkov and puts on the trench coat. While Nick puts on the coat, Cooper takes three black, wool ski-masks out of the package.

"How close are we?"

"Thirty seconds tops," Rogers reports.

"Good. Put this on."

He hands Temple a ski mask. Temple puts his on. Cooper dons his and hands one to Rogers who holds it his in teeth while he continues to drive.

"Snipers. Can't be too careful."

Nick knows the drill.

"SOP. Not a problem."

The car carrying Temple, Rogers, and Cooper skids to a stop at the entrance to the U.S. Mission. An MP walks over to the car as the three get out. Each one is wearing an identical black ski mask and black trench coat.

Karl Schuler sits on his folding stool peering through the scope of his sniper rifle. The rifle is supported by a folding tripod and is equipped with a silencer. A picture, a CIA employee head shot of Nick Temple, is propped up next to the rifle.

Schuler, thanks to having been given access to both frequencies and encryption codes, has been monitoring the comms between Dave Lacroix and the extraction teams, and now the moment has arrived.

Schuler sees three figures, all dressed identically, get out of the sedan. He looks up from his scope for just a second. He curses himself for not having charged more.

"He's going to get three for the price of one!" he thinks to himself.

Back to business. He lowers his head back down, takes aim through the scope, and squeezes off a round.

Cooper is hit by a round in the shoulder and falls to the ground. The MP, Temple, and Rogers immediately take cover behind the sedan. The car's windshield shatters from a second round. The scrambling MP reaches for his sidearm as he is hit by a third round from the sniper.

Two more MPs from the guard house run out to drag their fallen colleague to cover. One is hit in the leg by the sniper but continues to assist the rescue effort.

Temple and Rogers are pinned behind the car.

"If we don't get inside, he'll kill us all right here!"

Nick agrees. "Whenever you're ready."

Rogers turns to the MPs in the guard house and shouts.

"We're going in. Give us whatever suppression fire you can." The MPs, sidearms drawn, acknowledge. They pop up and return fire in the general direction of Schuler. One spots the silencer protruding from the window frame. They pour small arms fire into the building, but they know they are too far for their rounds to be effective. An MP crouching in the guardhouse reports into his hand held radio.

"We're taking sniper fire from the building across the street. Three are down. We need back up. Now!"

He drops the radio and joins the other MPs who are providing as much suppressing fire as they can.

As the MPs fire, Temple and Rogers scramble from behind the car towards the entrance. Rogers is hit immediately and falls wounded to the ground. Temple keeps running. He leaps over the waist high gate. Rounds hit the ground around him. His left forearm is hit, but he makes it into the building alive.

A patrol car skids to a stop in front of the guard house. Two MPs, the driver and one in the back seat, spill out of the passenger side doors using the car for cover. The MP from the back seat reaches back into the passenger compartment and pulls out a loaded M18 57mm recoilless rifle. He looks over to an MP in the guardhouse who points to

Schuler's sniper nest and shouts, "Fourth floor. Fifth window in from the right end of the building."

The MP with the M18 acknowledges with a thumbs up. In one motion, he gets on one knee, swings the weapon around so it is steadied on the trunk of the patrol car, finds the window frame, acquires his target through the M18's sight, and fires.

Schuler sees the MP swing the M18 into action. He drops his rifle as he scrambles for cover. As he dives behind one of the few walls of sheetrock in the apartment, the round from the weapon screams through the uncovered window, slams into an interior wall, and in an instant of white heat and exploding chaos obliterates the room and its contents, including Karl Schuler.

CHAPTER 66

TIME FOR A LITTLE MEET AND GREET

Temple rips off his ski mask. In spite of the wound to his left forearm he reloads the Makarov as he bounds up the stairs to the second floor. It's been more than two years since he was last in this building, but it appears to him that the interior's layout and functions are unchanged. Unsure where to start, he walks down the hall to a large conference room and enters.

Cornell Bailey is at the far end of the conference room. A large, oval conference table surrounded by leather chairs occupies the center of the room. A door diagonally across the room from where Nick just entered reminds him that there is another entrance to the room. The room is unchanged since 1956.

Bailey has a U.S. Army officer's standard issue Colt .45 pointed at Nick.

"Drop it, Temple."

Temple hesitates. Bailey fires off a round that whizzes past Temple's head and lodges in the wall behind him.

"The next one won't miss. Drop it!"

Temple drops the Makarov to the floor. He uses his empty right hand to place pressure on the wound to his left arm. A self-satisfied grin comes over Bailey's face.

"I guess this makes me a hero," he gloats.

Nick's not buying it.

"How do you figure?"

"Really? Figure it out. I've captured the biggest traitor of the Cold War. Nicholas Temple–defector!"

"You've got a big problem, Mr. Special Assistant."

"And how's that?"

"Think about it, asshole. How are you going to explain the fact that this dangerous defector strolled into the U.S. Mission in Berlin with the help of a CIA extraction team? Oh, and let's not leave out the fact that he was armed the entire time he was with the team and they all spent about half an hour of good buddy time shooting their way out of Commie land to get to an American sanctuary. Sound like your typical defector?"

Richardson and Johnson's beat up Chevy pulls up to the guard house just as an Army ambulance arrives. The MPs are tending to the wounded. Sirens in the distance indicate a civilian response to the burning, unfinished apartment complex.

Richardson and Johnson flash identification as they walk up to the MPs. A second ambulance arrives.

Johnson takes a quick look around and sees that Nick is not among the casualties.

"CIA. Anyone make it inside?

One of the MPs responds.

"One, I think."

Richardson and Johnson jump over the waist high gate and run towards the building's entrance.

Bailey stops laughing.

"You're an idiot. It doesn't matter what you are. It matters what people think you are. I can't decide if I should shoot you in the back–you know, shot while trying to escape–or make you turn around so that I look like Wyatt Fucking Earp."

"Profanity? You're slipping, Bailey."

"Let's get this over with. You want to confess before I kill you?"

"Sure. Ready?"

"Any time you are. You're a dead man either way."

Bailey pulls a small recorder out of his jacket pocket, switches it on and slides it on the conference to table to Nick. Nick picks it up and begins.

"Okay. I'll confess that this whole deal has been a set up. I'll confess that a roll of Minox film has about a dozen pictures from a KGB file belonging to Vasily Malenkov with your name all over it. I'll confess that the Director was in on the entire deal and sent me over here to try to get that information. I'll confess that your dumb ass is going to prison until the day of your execution for treason. You want more?"

Nick puts the recorder down on the conference room table.

Bailey, eyes bulging with fear, is instantly enraged.

"Liar!"

He raises his .45 to execute Nick just as the alternate entrance door opens.

The Director steps in. His hands are in the air, their palms facing Bailey to show that he has no weapon.

"Put it down, Cornell."

A look of panic comes over Bailey's face, but he quickly regains his composure.

"I've got him, sir. We can wrap this whole thing up right here, right now."

The Director puts his hands down.

"Forget it, Cornell. Can't you see you're finished?"

"I've got him. The traitor, sir. It's Temple, just as we suspected."

"Are you going to make me go through this, Cornell?"

"Sir?"

"The financials didn't tell us enough. They just pointed in your direction. We hoped Malenkov would have the rest."

Temple reaches into his breast pocket and pulls out the Minox.

"I hit the jackpot. You're cooked, buddy boy."

The Director pulls a tape recorder, identical to the one now holding Nick's "confession," from his pocket. He places it on the conference table and presses the play button. A conversation between Bailey and Natalie begins to play.

"And what do I do while you are off chasing spies? Maybe I'll give your wife a call. We could go shopping. We could swap stories over lunch."

"Wait for me. I'll call you after the dust settles."

"Cornell, how many times have you told me to wait? Do you think I'm stupid?"

Furious, Bailey waves his pistol at the Director.

"Turn it off, damn it! Turn it off."

He fires at the recorder. The shot misses. The Director calmly reaches out and turns it off.

Richardson and Johnson are on the bottom floor of the Mission Building. They hear the shot Bailey fired and bolt upstairs in the direction of the shot.

Bailey is frantic.

"Where did you get that?

"There's far more to Natalie than you imagined, my friend."

"Liar!"

"Why, Cornell? Why?"

Bailey is shouting now, unable to control either his fear or his rage. He's a mess.

"Why? Why? Ten years of being your lackey and you ask me why? You think I wanted to spend my whole life fetching things for you? I know more about the company than you'll ever know, but I was always second fiddle."

"It's not enough, Cornell. Not enough for treason. You don't like your job, you quit. You don't jump to the other side. You don't help them murder your countrymen!"

"It's enough to want to get the hell out from under you."

"You could have left any time."

Bailey is practically pleading now.

"Where was I going to go? Retire on some pathetic pension with my devoted and completely worthless wife? Live out some quiet life in the country? With what I know? I deserved better. I deserved more than you or anyone else was ever willing to give me."

The Director is disgusted by this man willing to sell out his country to salve his ego.

"You're pathetic."

"I had the key to the gold mine all along."

The Director thunders in response.

"Is that how you see this? Money? This is about money? What about your country? What about the trail of bodies, Cornell? This isn't just about your cozy goddam retirement with your slut of a mistress."

Temple has seen enough. He starts to walk towards Bailey to bring things to a head. Bailey, now in a full panic, points his weapon at Temple.

"Don't move!"

"You can't kill Temple and me, Cornell."

"The hell I can't. Temple kills you, I kill Temple. That's how it's going down. I'm the hero. Ha! I might even get your job."

"You're not getting anything except a firing squad, or, if you're lucky, the gas chamber. Drop it, Cornell."

"Never!"

Bailey starts to bring his weapon around to aim it at the Director. As he does, Johnson and Richardson burst in. Temple hits the ground and grabs his dropped Makarov. Bailey swings his weapon in the direction of the intrusion and fires wildly at Johnson and Richardson. The Director pulls a .45 from a shoulder holster and fires a round hitting Bailey in the back of the head. He is killed instantly. The firing stops, but the smell of gunpowder is trapped in the windowless room.

The Director walks over to Bailey, kneels down as if to feel for a pulse. With half of his head missing, there's no doubt that the traitor is dead. The Director stands up and puts his .45 back into his shoulder holster.

"Switchback, eh Temple?"

"Yes, sir. Seemed like it was worth a shot."

"Not our cleanest effort, but it'll do. God damn I hate field work. Let's get this mess cleaned up."

He walks out of the conference room. Temple, Richardson, and Johnson stare after him.

"Didn't know the old boy still had it in him," Richardson finally offers.

"Nice to see you Nick," Johnson adds.

"Believe me, it's great to see you fellas. Let's see if the MPs can use some help."

"How about some first aid on that arm?"

"It'll wait. You guys coming?"

"You have to ask?" Johnson responds.

The three men head out of the room to offer their assistance to their fellow Americans.

CHAPTER 67

LOOSE ENDS

Colonel Roznechenko sits at Malenkov's desk. He is dressed in his uniform and, as befits his mission, is wearing a sidearm. Malenkov, in handcuffs, is brought in by two Soviet soldiers. His face is bruised and swollen.

Roznechenko motions to the soldiers to remove the handcuffs.

"Sit, Vasily Ivanovitch, sit."

Once his handcuffs are removed, Malenkov reflexively rubs his sore wrists as he sits. Roznechenko opens the silver cigarette box on the desk, taps the cigarette, and lights it with the silver cigarette lighter.

"Can I offer you a cigarette?"

Malenkov decides he has nothing to lose by being defiant.

"I would be pleased to smoke one of my own cigarettes."

Roznechenko gives him a cigarette and lights it for him.

"That is what you don't understand, what you never understood, Vasily Ivanovitch. None of these things are yours. All of this belongs to the people of the Soviet Union. At any rate, we have decided that this building has outlived its usefulness and we will be making a gift of it to the people of the German Democratic Republic."

"Of course, Comrade Colonel. I am sure they will, as always, be pleased by our generosity."

"This business with Temple is unfortunate."

"It's the world we live in," Malenkov fatally offers.

Roznechenko explodes.

"How can you so easily dismiss your own absolute incompetence?"

Roznechenko rises from the desk and starts wandering around the room.

"The Americans have made us look like fools. Your failures have cost the Soviet Union a great deal."

"And you were sent here to deliver that message, a message I was able to presume from my arrest and subsequent beating?"

Roznechenko is now behind Malenkov, but Malenkov continues to look straight ahead, even when he addresses Roznechenko.

"I am much more than a delivery boy, Vasily Ivanovitch. Much more."

"Executioner too?"

"Finish your cigarette."

Malenkov takes a long drag on the cigarette, looks pensively at it for a moment, shrugs his shoulders and puts it out in what earlier that day was his ashtray sitting on his desk. He sits back in his chair as Roznechenko pulls out his pistol, aims it directly at the base of Malenkov's skull, and pulls the trigger. The impact from the round destroys Malenkov's head and throws his body to the floor. The report of the pistol causes Kropotkin to come running in. He grins as he stares at Malenkov's shattered skull and lifeless body. Roznechenko wipes the butt of his pistol off with his handkerchief and places the pistol in the limp hand of the dearly departed.

"Comrade Malenkov was so ashamed of his conduct in the

Temple affair that he decided to take his own life."

Kropotkin nods with approval.

"Remove the body. Do what you wish with the weapon. If anyone asks, tell them you took it from Malenkov's hand leaving no doubt about his cowardly suicide."

Kropotkin laughs. He picks up the weapon, admires it, and tucks it into his waistband.

"I'll have him dumped in River Spree."

Kropotkin bends over to pick up the body. Roznechenko moves back towards the chair behind the desk. He notices some blood on the chair which he wipes off with his handkerchief before he sits down.

A new receptionist comes in just as the soldiers are removing Malenkov's body.

"Bring me the file on Vanessa Porter."

"Yes, Comrade Colonel."

She exits. Roznechenko puts out his cigarette. He picks up the cigarette lighter, admires it for a moment, and, smiling, puts it in his pocket.

Three Soviet agents sit in a car on the street across from Vanessa Porter's apartment waiting for her to come out. It is two in the morning, and the street is otherwise deserted. A taxi cab pulls up in front of the apartment building. Vanessa Porter quickly steps out of the building and down its small flight of exterior stairs. A scarf covers her head, but the agents have no doubt that it's her. She carries a small, overnight bag. As she is about to reach the taxi at the curb, it suddenly speeds away. She freezes for just a moment before she starts to dash back inside the building. At the same moment two of the Soviet agents jump out of their car as the other executes a U-turn. The agents and the car arrive at the curb on her side of the street simultaneously.

Vanessa runs up the steps, into the apartment building. She tries to pull the door closed behind her, but one of the agents grabs the handle, flings the door open, and bolts inside after her with the other agent close behind.

Within seconds the agents remove Vanessa from the building. They carry her between them. She hangs limp and her feet drag. The agents stuff her into the back seat of the waiting car. They get in the car and speed away.

Less than a minute later, a dark green U.S. Army sedan with Nick Temple behind the wheel pulls up in front of Vanessa's apartment building.

Nick had tried without success to reach her after the shootout at the U.S. Mission. He left messages everywhere he could think of, but he couldn't find her. Vanessa, at home for the first time all day, got through to him at Berlin Brigade HQ. That was 15 minutes ago. She was in a panic. An old contact let her know that Malenkov was dead. With her "insurance policy" now worthless, she had to flee Berlin. Nick told her to wait for him, that he could guarantee her safe passage to the States.

Nick jumps out of his car, pulls a pistol out of his shoulder holster, and runs up the steps into the building, praying that he isn't too late. He nearly trips over Vanessa's overnight bag lying in the building's foyer. Taking three steps at a time, he bounds up the flight of stairs to

Vanessa's apartment and tries the door. It's unlocked. Not a good sign. Weapon drawn, he rushes into the empty apartment, runs into the bedroom, flicks on the lights and sees open dresser drawers indicating an attempted hasty escape. He quickly inspects the other rooms of the apartment. Finding nothing and no one, he runs back down the stairs, stops at the small overnight bag, opens it and inspects the contents. A U.S. passport with Vanessa's photograph and bearing the name Valerie Temple sits inside a pocket of the bag's lid. He stops searching. He knows she's gone, taken, and probably already dead.

Nick walks slowly out of the front door of the apartment building, his hands at his sides, defeated. He makes his way down the steps as if in a trance, gets into his car, and drives down the street into the cold depths of the Berlin night.

Natalie Kramer sits in her living room reading a magazine. The television is on in the background. She smokes. There is a knock at the door. She puts her magazine down, takes a drag from her cigarette, puts it out in an ashtray, and walks over to the door.

"Who is it?"

Instead of an answer, the door bursts open. Two men in black trench coats rush in. Natalie tries to run, but one of the men tackles her. As they struggle, the other man pulls out a pistol with a silencer on it. He aims carefully and pulls the trigger. The bullet hits Natalie in the head, killing her instantly. The man who tackled her stands up as the executioner checks for a pulse. He finds none, but just to make certain, he puts two more rounds in her disintegrating skull. He tosses the still-smoking weapon and it lands with a thud on her lifeless back. The two men leave the apartment, turning its lights off on their way.

Six West Berlin Polizei stand at the edge of the Spree River. The overcast day is cold with snow in the offing. Their vehicles are parked nearby with their flashing roof lights going. At their feet is a body covered with a sheet. One of them writes in a small note pad as the others smoke.

An unmarked black sedan with American military tags pulls up and parks near the group of policemen. An Army Major gets out of the front passenger seat. Nick Temple gets out of the back seat. He and the Major walk over to the body. The Major motions to one of the Polizei to pull the sheet back from the face of the body. It's a woman. She's naked. Her face is swollen from being in the water, and her throat has been slit from one ear to the other. Her dead eyes are open in horror.

Nick turns away. "It's her, Major."

"You're certain?"

Temple nods. He pulls out a cigarette and lights it. The Major motions to the Polizei to cover the bloated, distorted face of the once beautiful, but now late Vanessa Porter.

"I'm sorry, Mr. Temple. We should go."

The Major guides Temple back towards the sedan.

"Did you know her well?"

"Sure. But it was a long time ago."

The Army Major and Temple get back in the sedan, and the sedan drives away leaving the Polizei to gather the body and clear the scene.

CHAPTER 68

HOME AGAIN

The Director of Central Intelligence sits at his desk in Washington, D.C., poring over a file. He quickly flips through the pages of the thick file. Seated in front of him is a mid-level document analyst, who finds his first visit to the Director's office more than a bit intimidating. In spite of that, he knows the file is solid. He's been over it backwards and forwards, can recite it chapter and verse, and is ready for anything the Director throws at him. In short, he's completely over-prepared.

The Director closes the file and looks up.

"Is there anything else? Anything not in this file that should come to my attention?"

"It's all right there, sir. I think the executive summary lays it out pretty clearly."

"It does indeed. Nice work."

The Director pushes a button on his intercom.

"Cheryl, I need to speak to the President."

The analyst, thrilled that his work will be center of a discussion between two of the planet's most powerful men, recognizes his cue to leave.

"If you'll excuse me then, sir."

"Of course. Be sure you're immediately available for the next 24 hours. Let my secretary know where you plan to be. Wherever it is, don't get too far from a phone. You might have to do some pitching on this thing with the higher ups."

"With pleasure, sir."

The analyst leaves as the Director contemplates his meeting with the President.

An unmarked FBI sedan pulls up in front of Bill Johnson's house. Bill Johnson and Kyle Richardson are in the back seat.

"All right, then. This is my stop. See you at the office?"

"Count on it."

"Nice work, by the way."

"We're a good team, the three of us."

"Agreed."

They shake hands and Johnson gets out of the car. Peggy Johnson bursts out of the front door, runs over to her husband, and they embrace as the sedan pulls away from the curb.

Temple, whose face still shows some signs of his recent ordeal, walks gingerly towards his office. His secretary looks up with pride and affection. She is well aware of the beating his career has taken of late. In her view, the Company treated him unfairly. She is also well aware of the fact that his recent successful mission has resuscitated both his career and hers.

Temple stops at her desk and pulls a stack of mail and messages out of an "In Box." He goes through the stack slowly, silently.

"Terry, hold my calls for the rest of the day."

"Yes, Mr. Temple."

Temple starts to head to his office when his secretary speaks up.

"Mr. Temple."

He stops and turns.

"It's good to see you, sir."

"Thanks. It's good to be back, Terry."

"The Director's secretary called, sir. He'd like to meet with you at your earliest convenience."

"At my convenience?"

"That's how she put it, sir."

"Should I make him sweat?"

"I think not, sir."

"Yeah, bad idea. Okay, call her and tell them I'm on my way."

The Director sits at his desk. He is writing notes on a legal pad, notes that will serve as the outline for his briefing of the Commander in Chief and the other members of his national security team. The briefing is set for 8 a.m. in the Oval Office.

His intercom buzzes, followed immediately by his secretary's voice.

"Mr. Temple to see you, sir."

"Fine. Send him right in."

The Director gets up from behind his desk as Temple enters the office. He greets Nick warmly with a handshake.

"Getting settled back in?"

"Oh, sure. Nothing to it, sir."

"Good. Have you seen these? They came by courier today. The contact's a solicitor in London."

The Director lifts a manila folder off his desk and hands it to Nick. He opens it and goes through a handful of the documents in the folder, shaking his head as he quickly scans them.

"First time I've seen these. I suspected she wasn't telling me everything."

"I had an analyst look at them. There's no doubt they confirm what we already knew. Why do you suppose she held back?"

"That was just her way, sir, in everything."

"I understand you were close."

The Director knows damn well they were close. For six months he was getting reports about how "close" they were until he finally ordered Temple to break it off. Nick isn't surprised by the Director's choice of language. It's natural for him to want to create the impression of distance from events that speak to the dark side of what his agents do.

"I'd rather not go into it, if you don't mind, sir."

"Quite right. I simply wanted to say that I am sorry she's dead. Let's leave it at that."

"Fair enough."

The Director's desk phone rings. He pushes the flashing button on his phone and picks up the receiver. His lips tighten and his eyes narrow to slits as he listens. He takes a deep breath before speaking.

"Kiev? How many? . . . All right. Temple's already here. I want you in my office in 5 minutes."

He hangs up the phone, sits down in his chair and motions for Temple to do the same.

"The sons of bitches didn't learn their lesson. Here we go again. Get your boys together, Nick. The three of you just got a promotion."

THE END

www.ingramcontent.com/pod-product-compliance
Lightning Source LLC
Chambersburg PA
CBHW070622130626
46556CB00001B/447